CW00521788

DAVID PALIN lives in Berkshire and is a writer of dark, psychological thrillers. His first book containing two short novels, *For Art's Sake* and *In The Laptops Of The Gods,* was published in 2006. Three eBooks followed.

David has collaborated as editor and co-writer for various authors, for example Greg Taylor's *Lusitania R.E.X*, as well as producing screen treatments and screenplays for writers whose novels have sparked potential interest from film producers. His own screenplay of *For Art's Sake* is in the process of being pitched for a movie.

This Changed Everything

First published in 2018 by
Nine Elms Books
Unit 6B
Clapham North Arts Centre
26–32 Voltaire Road
London SW4 6DH
Email: inquiries@bene-factum.co.uk
www.bene-factum.co.uk

ISBN: 978-1-910533-37-6
Epub: 978-1-910533-38-3

Copyright © David Palin. Protected by copyright under the terms of the
International Copyright Union.

The rights of David Palin to be identified as the author of this work have
been asserted by him in accordance with the Copyright, Designs and Patents
Act, 1988. All rights reserved.

This book is sold under the condition that no part of it may be reproduced,
copied, stored in a retrieval system or transmitted in any form or by any means,
electronic, mechanical, photocopying, recording or otherwise without prior
permission of the author.

Cover design: Tony Hannaford
Book design: Dominic Horsfall

Set in Borgia Pro
Printed in the UK

*This is a work of fiction. Names, characters, businesses, places, events and incidents are either
the products of the author's imagination or used in a fictitious manner. Any resemblance to
actual persons, living or dead, or actual events is purely coincidental.*

THIS CHANGED EVERYTHING

DAVID PALIN

NINE
ELMS

My thanks must go David Imrie for his patience and attention to detail as an editor, to Susan Mears for introducing me to Anthony Weldon of Nine Elms Books and to him for giving me the opportunity to publish this book.

I

It was written in the air that something bad was going to happen that evening, but looking back, when it was all too late, Claire Treloggan realised her state of heightened anxiety hid from her the coming storm.

Even when the late November wind pounced as she re-emerged from the clinic, tangling her hair and throwing her off balance for a moment, she just pulled on the coat she'd gone back in to collect, put her head down and made her way back to the car. Forgetting to pick up that coat on a night like this further illustrated that her mind was elsewhere. Likewise, the chill rattling of the early Christmas lights registered only on a subconscious level with her as they swung with a distinct lack of goodwill in the gusts. For her, just for the moment, terror was the prospect of giving birth, even though it was seven months away. Perhaps she had hoped attending that afternoon's early baby-care class might help; how wrong she had been! Clearly her brain was already frying; what the hell had she been thinking, or rather not thinking, when she decided to go along?

Only as she approached the car did she start to take heed of her surroundings. The last stubborn flesh of autumn was being stripped from the trees by a buffeting, biting north wind, and the clattering branches veined a full moon, across which, from time to time, the silhouettes of shredded clouds capered; reeling witches at a Sabbath. Pieces of litter pranced like springboks, mocking the emptiness of the high street while leaves skittered across the paving stones in short, scraping bursts, hurrying to their doom in damp gutters and against kerbs. Yet even though the town, like much of the Cornish peninsula, was devoid of tourists and mostly closed down for the winter, there was something else present; a charge in that space between heaven and earth that we call our world; intangible, but undeniable; enough to make the hairs stand up on the back of Claire's neck, even though most of mankind had buried its sixth sense long ago in the name of progress.

She hurried into the car, closed the door, but the ensuing silence troubled her ears more than the howling wind, so she opened the window a touch. She glanced at the clock on the dashboard; not yet 5pm. It felt wrong, being on the road home at this hour, but she would have to get used to it when her time came to make the dreaded school run. Though it irked her having to sacrifice her career in the short term for domesticity, one of Richard's conditions – an interesting word – was that this would be no latch-key kid. As she was hoping this baby would strengthen her marriage, it seemed impetuosity, otherwise known as spreading her legs after a drink too many, had led her down a cul-de-sac.

Her marriage. Didn't that phrase, suggesting a unilateral arrangement, just sum up how distant they had become, despite the fact that they wanted to love each other? As for conditions, why hadn't she imposed a few of her own? On reflection, it appeared she had failed to see some of the road signs at the start of their relationship; clearly she'd missed the "No Exit" sign at the entrance to this particular street.

The trouble was, as far as her career was concerned, that things moved on apace all the time in marketing, particularly in this age of social media. Months spent away might mean years catching up again. Having fallen pregnant at thirty-five, would she have those years? She knew she would need to stay abreast of developments during maternity leave; what she didn't know was whether she had the will, or the energy. Plus, she was a disciple of the dogma: *employ people good enough to replace you*. Of course, her position would have to be held open, but plenty of damage could be done in her absence. She'd have to make sure she left no troubled waters on which her second-in-command, one of those 'run ten miles a night, skinny is the new power ponytail, lunch is for yesterday' belladonnas, could pour oil in her absence.

There was another problem; one of far greater concern for Claire. She put her hand on her stomach, and the negative thoughts accompanying that gesture would have been considered heretical by the Stepford mothers-to-be with whom she had just spent a wasted hour.

A gust of wind snorted in derision as it swooped past her cracked-open window. It startled her. There were still seven months left to get worked up over this; what the hell state would her nerves be in after that? She turned the ignition key and pulled out of the car park with perhaps rather more revs than usual, to start the journey back along the coast road, a winding route which required you to have your wits about you whatever the time or season, never mind when black clouds were overshadowing your mind on a darkening winter evening that seemed in the mood for mischief.

Distracted by thoughts of what lay ahead – in all senses – Claire failed to notice what was behind her.

****

She felt the irritation rising again as she drove along. It didn't matter what the specialists said about breathing; Claire couldn't imagine that anything would anaesthetise the pain of the birth. Right now, coarse comparisons like 'shitting a melon' and 'trying to push a piano through a cat-flap' were the only images that seemed to resonate.

Nor could the trite clichés, mouthed with such readiness by earth-mothers in the clinic that afternoon about the *miracle* growing inside her, disguise the fact that her troubles were only just beginning; sleep-deprivation, intellectual stagnation, bags under the eyes. Richard had been so keen to start a family; she wished she could transfer some of those delights to him!

There was no avoiding the truth; choice had now gone out of the window. She was saddled worse than a barge-horse; her time, her money, her life – they would never be her own again. And what about her brain? How long before it atrophied and she caught herself talking about the price of Pampers? Years before, when she was on a two-year secondment in France, she had stopped going to the British Women's Club after most of its members, predominantly wives who had come over because of their husbands' careers, had taken the opportunity to start a family; their conversation seemed to descend with depressing reliability to the intellectual level of the thing they had spawned.

Ah yes – her time in France. The memories returned with an almost visceral quality, of a time when she had been, on reflection, without a care in the world. Had she fully appreciated it? Just as youth is wasted on the young, could the same be said of Paris? Back then she – they – had seen it as fortunate that Richard was also able to organise a placement with his own company to coincide with hers. Now, with the combined burdens of expectation, the future and the womb weighing her down, the questions raged. Had it been a good thing that he came out with her? Worse still – here she placed her hand on her stomach in a reflex that spoke little of nurture and more of dread – had Richard resented her career? Was she imagining it, or did his talk of family start not long after that? Did he decide that the only acceptable conclusion to her time of *Liberté* and *Egalité* was *Paternité*?

Lost inside her state of distraction, she couldn't remember the exact point at which the lights behind her started to give concern. Had they been following her since she left town? She wasn't sure. The fact that they hadn't tried to overtake her was not really an issue – after all this was a dangerous stretch of road; the carnivorous, frothing jaws of the north Cornish coast waited for anyone misjudging the snaking bends and there were dips obscuring oncoming vehicles. Suddenly the Freelander felt even more big and cumbersome on the narrow band of tarmac. It was their spare car and, somewhat inconveniently, her own Qashqai seemed to have developed a problem with the brakes, so Richard had taken it in for repairs that morning. The car behind appeared to be keeping pace with her even though she had already taken one chance to speed up.

"Just let him past," she muttered to herself and applied gentle pressure to the brakes. Her assumption that it was a man told her all she needed to know about her state of mind.

The lights slowed. Then they flashed, and Claire found herself with an unwanted passenger – fear.

She picked up speed again. Her pursuer followed suit. For a moment she wondered whether she should stop. After all, though she had few neighbours – it was more a loose gathering of houses than a village – it might have been one of them trying to warn her that she had something like a faulty rear light. Then Claire found herself laughing; a derisive sound. "Yup, good comedy moment there," she said out loud. "Let's stop on this isolated stretch of road so that the man driving so freakily behind me can…".

The lights flashed once more. There had to be an innocent explanation. After all, if this guy was trying to follow her, would he have wanted to draw attention to himself?

"Unless he wants to scare you to death first". The words were out before she could prevent them, as if some sprite was determined to express what she was trying to avoid.

Now Claire weighed up her options. The next turning left would take her towards home, along a single-track road with passing places. The pursuer wouldn't be able to overtake her, but at the house she'd have to wait for the electronic gates to open; never the quickest of operations, but ten times slower when your mind was travelling an even darker lane. And even if he – because by now she had no doubt it was a man – drove on by, she'd still have led him right to her door and she had seen enough horror movies, with women fumbling for their keys while snatching terrified glances over their shoulders, not to want to go through that every time she came home in the dark.

The lights flashed again; and again.

He was getting impatient. Perhaps that was a good thing. What was it her friend Freddy had said? *An angry psychopath makes mistakes. It's the calculating, reptilian ones you have to fear.* Then she remembered the context of his comment; they make mistakes, leaving forensic evidence at murder scenes. As cold comforts went, that one had been picked out from the back of the freezer.

She made her decision, drove on past the turning for home, though not without a huge surge of regret, and carried on along the coast road, speeding up before making a sudden dive off left at the next turning, a little used back lane, in the hope of losing her pursuer.

There was only darkness now in the rear-view mirror. She puffed out her cheeks.

Perhaps this was the time to get off the road, kill her lights and just hide. But no; forest was springing up on either side and she felt sure she would get stuck, making herself a sitting duck, or kill herself colliding with a tree. So she accelerated instead. The trunks of the trees were stark columns in the beams of the headlights, forcing her down a tunnel into the blackness beyond. The pounding anger of waves against cliffs had been left behind and she was passing through a world of stillness that was much more menacing.

"Shit!" she hissed. "Shit! Shit! Shit!"

Behind her, the opening down which she'd shot was visible again, and she saw what she had been dreading, as two points of light turned into it, caught up with dreadful haste and efficiency, and then took their now-accustomed place behind her – except there was a furious flashing now, as if enough was enough.

She thought about calling the police and then dismissed the idea. The Freelander was an older model and had none of the communication features which had become standard in recent years. Though not lacking confidence as a driver, Claire dreaded to think of the consequences of her trying to make a call on this thin strip of concrete with no hands-free. Besides, what would she say to the police, or Richard for that matter? *"There's a car on the road behind me."* Perhaps this was just another car impatient to get past. How did she know it was the same driver?

She just knew.

Claire remembered this densely-wooded lane ran for three miles or so until it linked up with the main road to St Ives. That was it for her now; only one choice remained. She had to stay ahead and get to that main road first. It was a straight run for the line. The reward – her life perhaps?

There were no houses, or even a pub, along the lane; that she knew of anyway. For the first mile no headlights came towards her. Wrong time of day; school-run over; the working day still drawing to a weary close.

Then, at a point where the road widened to accommodate one of the passing places, her pursuer lost patience and shot past her. He'd been toying with her, knowing his car was powerful enough to overtake at any half chance; she noticed through her veil of fear that it was a BMW. If he had been enjoying terrifying her then that only made the situation worse, impossible though that seemed. Now he screeched to a halt, about thirty feet ahead, angling his car to block the road.

Claire had long ago flipped the central locking switch, and though her instinct was to run, wild horses couldn't have dragged her from the car. She cut her lights to be able to see better, but there was no sign of any other car approaching from behind or from the opposite direction down the long straight road. The darkness of the woods overwhelmed her in no time and she flicked the lights on again. She toyed with reversing away, but it had never been a strong point of her driving, and if she ended up over the verge she would be helpless.

The driver leapt from his car. It seemed that speed was suddenly of the essence for him now; he couldn't rely on a continued absence of traffic. As he advanced, Claire realised with horror that, on this night of limited choices, her only one now might be to run him over.

"Oh God! Oh God!" she muttered. Could she do it? He didn't look psychotic – but that was always the way, wasn't it? *Think Ted Bundy* – she obeyed her own instruction, making matters worse. But she was going to have to do something, because he was nearly at the car.

Claire felt a simultaneous chilling of her blood and warming of her legs as her bladder gave way...

...not at the sight of the other driver, but at the menacing hiss of the words from the seat behind her.

2

"I guess the death of my sister was when it really hit it home – just how different I was from most other people."

He noted the way the PhD student, a guy only a few years older than him, but wearing a tweed jacket from a lost genera-tion, glanced at the pre-session questionnaire. Was that a kind of nervous tic – he must have known that revelation wasn't on there – or was that observation in itself a perfect example of misery seeking company?

Either way, this session needed to be a two-way thing; mutu-ally beneficial. He wasn't here just to be a test-case; assist someone privileged in achieving their doctorate. He needed this unbur-dening, whether there was help to be had or not.

"I'm sorry to hear that. How did she die?"

"She was murdered."

Again a startled scanning of the reference sheet. "There's no mention…"

"There really wasn't a tick-box that seemed appropriate."

The postgrad gave a thin smile, which, under the circum-stances, spoke of supreme awkwardness. He seemed to consider something for a moment and then placed the clipboard to one side. Now he sat back, tenting his fingers.

"Why exactly are you here?" There was no belligerence in the question, despite the passive aggression of his subject's previous response.

"There was a request on the Students' Union board."

"Yes, for potential case studies for the negative influence of emotions on dyadic negotiation."

"Well, once I'd looked it up and found it meant dealing with other people, I saw a place for me in that study. So…study away."

The postgrad was motionless now, perhaps angry that his time may have been wasted, but already professional enough to avoid betraying that anger through his body language or demeanour. His voice remained even, his pupils no more dilated than before. "Perhaps you would like to elucidate; explain to me why or how your sister's mur…death relates to this?"

Straight away it seemed to grow darker. It was nothing to do with the south-west skies. Exeter's campus remained bathed in unseasonable sunlight. Yet somehow it felt like the only things missing were candles and a confessional screen.

"I suppose from a very young age I've always been a little puzzled by the stranger in the mirror."

The postgrad couldn't prevent himself from sitting up straight, but he resisted interrupting.

"I was too young to consider it abnormal. Then there were the comments from my small and decreasing bunch of school friends, in the main regarding my failure to recognise them under circumstances where their behaviour or clothing changed; for example if we met out of school and therefore not in uniform.

"Mostly, the ribbing I received was mild enough – they likened me to an old man, absent-minded and forgetful – unlike the bully of our year, who smashed me around the head for not letting him into the lunch queue a day or so after he'd issued a similar warning. Puberty's a bitch; he'd shaved off his bum-fluff beard and I just didn't recognise him. "But you know how it is, particularly when you've just hit your teens. You hide what makes you different."

The postgrad nodded, again said nothing.

"You cope; have stratagems. It's the others that are weird, not you. I learned to pick out their weirdness – they would probably have just called it individuality – and use it to find markers; glasses, colour or cut of hair, tattoos, moles, type of belt and so on."

He paused, noticed how the postgrad's fingers had moved, despite his best efforts to remain neutral, from tented to clasped; white knuckled. Was he gripped, and, if so, genuinely or just by the possibility of a little extra spice for his doctorate paper?

In response to the demanding silence, he continued: "Anyway, there's banter from schoolmates, a bash round the head from the school bully, but these things are as nothing when you stare at a police line-up and cannot identify a man you've seen close up and believe killed your sister."

No clasping or tented fingers now; no pretence, just a sharp intake of breath. The postgrad leaned forward, elbows on knees. "My God!" He seemed to be considering. "Please forgive me for asking…" he glanced across at the questionnaire' "ah, I wish I knew your name."

"Probably as well you don't."

"Indeed." He raised a hand, took a deep breath, sat back again and continued. "I was going to ask you if you wanted to carry on, but I know you do. My question of why you're here has been more than answered." Now he fell silent again and waited.

"I knew something was wrong, just from how he was hurrying along."

"Who?"

He needed to ignore the interruption. "Back along the clifftop path towards me. I could hear the sea raging against the rocks far below. Although the sun was starting to dip, I still noticed the white strip on his wrist where a watch had been, visible below a shirt cuff that was missing a button and flapping open.

"He kept his head down and hurried on by. I found myself watching how he walked. Of course, I suspect now this wasn't purely subconscious.

"I knew from the colour of his shirt, a sort of rust shade, that it was him."

"Who?" There was some frustration in the question this time.

"The man my sister... the man Anna had been arguing with down a side-street, a little distance from the school. I'd gone looking for her as we sometimes walked home together, but when I turned up she told me to go away, though slightly less politely than that."

"Did you know why they were arguing; overhear anything?"

"As I came round the corner I saw why. His hand had been wandering towards forbidden territory; forbidden at that place and time anyway. He still had his watch on the offending wrist then. Looked to be worth a bit too."

The postgrad sat up a little. "So are you saying she..." he paused, "...how can I put this – knew him?"

"If you mean in a biblical sense I'd love to say no. However, my sister was bright, passionate, older than her years, and not for no reason is Poldark set in Cornwall."

Once again the PhD student didn't seem to know whether he should smile or not at the dark humour. On many fronts, the narrative was tip-toeing along a path every bit as fragile and fraught as an eroding coastal trail. However, he chose to stay quiet.

"Anyway, they had marched off arguing and I saw them making their way up to the cliff-top path, he trailing a bit behind her and seeming to remonstrate. I decided to wait a few minutes; eavesdropping on their anger was not as appealing as avoiding my sister's teenage wrath.

"Later, when the guy came back past me – let's call him Bill for no particular reason...

"Why?"

He ignored him. "...I, too, hurried along; first to the point where you could see the route snaking ahead for some distance before it became lost in the undulations of the land. There was no sign of Anna, no sign of anyone; no hikers at that time of day. Only the ragged edge of the cliffs and the silent, stony silhouette of a disused tin mine broke the sweep of the Cornish coast blending distantly into the sky. Now I raced to where flimsy netting and a sign warned of the trail's proximity to the edge; where the Atlantic is winning its long fight with the land.

"I didn't find her – but the authorities did, twenty-four hours later, washed up by some rough seas near Trebarwith Strand."

The postgrad was sitting forward. His face was hidden for a moment where his side-parted hair had fallen across it. Doubtless he wasn't considering, at that moment, that the hair, rather than the features re-emerging from behind it, would have been the badge by which his interlocutor might have recognised him under other circumstances. For now, and for him, it was simply a shield behind which he struggled to find anything to say.

At last he had something: "Are you sure it was Bill who…" he tutted in exasperation, "…ah, forget that question. Why would he be hurrying back otherwise without her and without asking for help?"

"Well, I suppose they could have argued and she stormed off, but I would have seen her heading home, even in the winter gloaming.

"Of course that's where I ran to next, told my parents, learnt that I was supposed to be my sister's keeper, even though she was older than me. I learnt also that my troubles were only just beginning."

The postgrad shook his head. "Of course! If we're talking about what I think we are with you, you wouldn't have been able to describe his face to the police anyway. Bloody hell!" Now he switched from shaking his head to nodding. "And that's why he needs a name, isn't it? Without some label, he is just a collection of pieces to you." He raised a hand as if in apology. "But we'll come back to that. Please continue."

"To this day, I have no idea whether the perpetrator was in the line-up they put together. All five men were wearing the type of rust-coloured shirt I'd described, but I suspect they'd been put in them by the police to help me. Whether they were all guys with records, I don't know. What I do know is, police efficiency hadn't extended to ripping off the cuff button so that I could look for a tan line from a missing watch. And why would it? I hadn't given them that detail. You learn to hide your problems and it becomes hard to let the mask slip. Instead, like a fool, I just kept doing what everyone said and studied the faces. I could no more explain about the shirt-cuff than I could demand that five angry looking men stuffed into a small room be made to walk up and down so that I could look for that slightly scuttling gait." He felt a sudden urge to laugh, perhaps for comic relief, and it infected his next words. "There was so little space in the line-up room; it would have been like some grotesque silent comedy.

"*'But he walked right past you'*, I heard my father say."

The postgrad was leaning forward again on his elbows. "This is fascinating stuff." Then he seemed to remember the context. "Tragic. Was he ever brought to justice?"

"I believe so."

"You don't know?"

"What I don't know is whether it's a part of my condition that I've somehow compartmentalised a lot of that episode and the intervening years till I saw your request for volunteers." He grinned; a rictus he knew didn't reach his eyes, but reflected a certain part of his soul. "You should have charged me a fee."

The postgrad leaned back in his chair. "Maybe one day I will."

"I take it then that our session is over."

"Not unless you want it to be. I need an espresso – would you like one? My feeling is we've only scratched the surface."

"You might be right – and yes please to a coffee."

The postgrad rose and headed over to a Nespresso maker. "When Professor Dowker based me in in his room I had to insist I be allowed to bring this." He patted the machine. "Anyway, forget the specific limits of my doctorate; I feel we can help each other here."

"Again, very probably. I'd say any boy who arrives at the spot where he believes his sister was just murdered, finds what might be the crucial piece of evidence, and hurls that watch right there and then into the oblivion of the Atlantic – yeah, he probably does need some help."

3

The touch of his fingertips on her neck made her shudder and she stiffened; awaited the reprisals – the frustrated anger.

Under the circumstances, it was little wonder that the buzz of the intercom made her jump out of her crawling skin.

However, the *tut* of irritation from Richard was something of a Pavlovian reaction, since the visitor wasn't exactly disturbing an enjoyable evening; one which, like so many, had been frosty from the moment she'd arrived home. This time though, there had been a particular awkwardness, from her side at least, when she had returned from another impromptu and off-the-record session with Freddy. She'd collected the baby from her mother and come back to lit candles, strawberries, chocolates on the table alongside champagne and soul on the music system. All this and a husband who was not away on business after all; had said that just to surprise her with a romantic evening. Her heart had gone out to him, interrupting its journey long enough to sink. She had gestured towards the child in her arms; never the best precursor to foreplay. "I'll just take her up to bed," she had said, wishing she could stand for him to do the same to *her*.

And that had been the way of it. She had tried – these days, allowing Richard to lift her hair and touch her neck counted as trying – but as soon as she had shut her eyes the demons had come at her again, out of the darkness. Medication and then her refusal to be beaten had just about given her back control over her sleeping hours. Anyway, her mind had chosen to draw a curtain across the finer details of the attack itself almost from the moment it ended, but her nerve endings and her skin, it seemed, couldn't forget. But who was she kidding? Even that balmy night on holiday in San Francisco, the night of Cissie's conception, had been the exception rather than the rule. The dry-rot in her physical relationship with her husband had set in long before the dreadful events of that November evening a year ago. He had sacrificed, too readily for her liking, the honed body of the sports-nut he'd once been. But what bugged her most was what the early middle-aged spread symbolised; he'd stopped caring. What stupidity had led her to entertain the notion that a child might heal things?

Worse though was the reality of *who* she had allowed to convince her. She had buried her head in the sand, refusing to face the possibility that in the arms of another she might be made whole again; not immediately, but sooner.

She wanted to blame Richard for how the marriage felt; the alternative was too distressing to contemplate. So the issues had been surfacing again, their stilted dialogue a precursor to icy foreplay; the latter mirroring their life together – a series of cautious steps through a minefield.

And now the intercom was buzzing.

Richard got off the sofa with reluctance, taking his glass with him, as he wandered up to the door and looked at the security screen. "I don't believe it," he muttered. "It's him again."

"Who?" asked Claire, trying to keep hope from her voice and confusion from her thoughts.

"Our favourite detective, Columbo."

Claire frowned in response.

"Fucking Logan." Richard glanced at his watch. "I mean, it's half past-bloody-seven."

"Well, Columbo's hardly a good analogy; Ben's always so…"

"…smart. Yes, I know." Richard downed the remaining contents of his champagne glass. "Like a bloody mannequin with a blue-flashing light. And whose benefit do you think that's for?" He stared at the screen again and made no attempt to conceal his sarcasm. "Wonder why he's on his own."

She tried to ignore him and ventured: "Maybe there's been some new turn of events."

"Well, if there has it's taken long enough."

"Richard, he's the Detective Chief Inspector. He co-ordinates the case. He controls the day-to-day investigation. He's there to help us get through this."

She saw Richard glance around the room, taking in the chocolates, the strawberries and the candles. "Well he's failing on all fronts then, isn't he?"

"That's not fair."

He looked long and hard at her. "Isn't it?" The hurt must have shown in her eyes, because his own softened. "Sorry."

"'Kay." There was a catch in her throat that shortened the word, but the surprise was that it came from seeing his pain.

"Suppose I'd better let him in."

To her shame, Claire felt a sudden panic, not wanting Ben Logan to see this scene of seduction. For a mad moment she even contemplated blowing out the candles. What was wrong with her?

It was a good few seconds before she heard the tyres crunch on the gravel outside. Claire had always found the long driveway of their house a little unnerving after dark, having grown up in the tight, twisting backstreets of Mevagissey, with the comfort of lit windows close at hand. The lurking presence of the breathing, sighing sea, out of sight because their house sat in a slight hollow, but never less than intimidating as it fought against the cliffs beyond their back gate, added to a sense of brooding menace; the north coast was wilder and more threatening than the gentle, sheltered south where she had been brought up. But Richard had insisted.

The house, with its five bedrooms, was way too large for them. Claire had always assumed it was all to do with status, but since falling pregnant she'd found herself wondering whether there had been a plan. She placed a hand on her stomach. Build it and they will come. This remote, iron-gated citadel had already started to feel like a prison, even before the attack had added an element of agoraphobia, forcing her to stay where she felt trapped.

Maybe she needed a hero. In stepped Logan, and, despite all she'd been through, Claire couldn't deny that her pulse quickened. As his dark eyes looked out from under nervous, downcast brows her blood seemed to rush to her lower abdomen, even if there was a saurian quality to that look from time to time; perhaps because of it.

****

As he walked into the lounge, Ben Logan couldn't help noticing a fourth presence there; discord. He needed none of his peculiar cognitive processes to pick up on it straight away and nor was he proud of the frisson of jealousy as he took in the soft lighting and music.

"Claire…Mrs Treloggan," he corrected himself, feeling awkward, the more so as he found himself straightening his tie. She looked, as she always did, wounded and gorgeous. He knew he should have been ashamed of harbouring these thoughts; that they, or a corrupted version of them, had arisen in a sick, short-circuiting mind a year before, finding ultimate expression in the premature shadows beneath Claire's blue eyes. Was there pain behind them? He had to assume so. But what could he do – within the bounds of the law at least?

Still, he preferred to think of himself as a gene closer to redemption, rather than one away from damnation. Some things were put on this earth to enhance its beauty and she was one of them. Even on the day he first interviewed her, just after he had engineered his promotion to Detective Chief Inspector and stepped in to take over the case from his inept predecessor, his notes – the off-the-record ones at least – suggested he had been mesmerised by her vulnerable allure. That had been only a couple of weeks after her ordeal, and his guilt had left him feeling that he should go home and find a hair shirt to pull on; because the craven thought had crossed his mind that, pregnant and trauma-tized though she was, some dark corner of his soul understood why this had happened to Claire Treloggan.

He'd had to focus hard; stand back and let the Ben Logan who could actually be trusted by victims resurface to help Claire get through her trauma. The problem was he didn't like that Ben Logan all that much sometimes. Promotion had come at more of a cost than he had anticipated; that business in Hampshire that had led to it had further shaken his faith in women and in his own judgement. The conspiratorial silence of ambition had been filled with the voice of his conscience and had taken its share of his sleep in the year since. Did he need Claire to redress that balance?

"So, to what do we owe the pleasure, Sergeant?" asked Richard, with unfortunate wording under the circumstances.

"Detective Chief Inspector," corrected Logan for possibly the hundredth time. The guy really was a prick and he gave no silent apology for *that* thought. He stood fidgeting with his signet ring, turning it round and round; a new tic he hated, but couldn't prevent. "I just wanted to give you an update."

Claire stood and gestured to a chair. "Please, sit down." She gave a nervous pull at the hem of her polo-neck jumper, straight-ening it, giving inadvertent emphasis both to the flatness of her stomach and the roundness of her breasts.

"It's okay, thank you." Logan smiled. "This won't take long."

"Presumably because there isn't much to tell," said Richard, who made his way a little unsteadily to the drinks cabinet and now poured himself a large single malt; single in all senses as the offer did not extend to the visitor, nor indeed to Claire.

Logan gave only the slightest of pauses, containing nonetheless a huge measure of self-control. "We've had a bit of a breakthrough."

"Really?" Claire and Richard spoke in unison, but the words seemed to come from such different places.

"This time it's significant." He addressed Claire now. "You remember I mentioned a couple of days ago on the phone that I'd revisited the scene of the crime? It's always been my way. I like to go back once all the dust has settled…"

"It's still swirling in the air as far as we're concerned," interrupted Richard. "Who knows whether we'll ever be able see the way ahead again?"

"Yes, I remember," said Claire. Her tone was conciliatory, as if trying to balance out her husband's cynicism. "You mentioned some fibres."

Richard took a large gulp of whiskey and then pointed rather dismissively using the hand that held the glass. "Ah yes, Claire did say something. Wasn't going anywhere, if I understood correctly."

Logan saw the two of them exchange glances. Though the exact nature of those escaped him, he believed he could have taken an educated guess. He pushed on, aware of Richard's mushrooming cynicism, perhaps because of it, and all the time wondering whether his feelings were quite objective.

"As I say, my modus operandi is to hope something will reveal itself if I open myself up to that possibility; try to commune with the devil, as it were." He glanced at Claire, hoped her silence wasn't disapproval and pushed on. "Back at the spot where your attacker had driven the car, further along in the quarry where he set it alight, I remembered that the team had found one partial footprint in a patch of wet earth. Mostly, the high winds had dried the ground, but in that partial print, there were some fibres; carpet fibres, to be precise."

"I see," said Richard. Again he waved his glass in Logan's general direction, though he seemed to avoid eye contact. "So we're looking for someone with a carpet."

Logan continued to mask his irritation. He glanced at Claire and saw something that might have been understanding, perhaps even empathy, in the tilt of her head; enough to help him to keep the lid on his temper. "I'm not quite sure how this got overlooked when the crime scene was first examined, but," he paused, "somehow it did, for which I offer deepest apologies on behalf of my predecessor. Maybe the guys in Forensics were too focussed on the car wreck itself, assuming it had been burnt to hide evidence." As no-one seemed to know what to say to that, he ploughed on. "Anyway, the fibres looked one thing, or rather nothing special, under the normal laboratory lighting tests that were done a year ago. However, when I went back to the scene last week it occurred to me to wonder whether we should have done a fluorescent analysis on them, so I ordered one and the results I got back today are quite another thing"

"You could have told us this over the phone."

"Yes, Mr Treloggan, but as I said this is real progress and I wanted to share it face-to-face. The carpet in question was never for sale to the general public. It was expensive and effectively produced to order for a very limited market – a company restoring and selling classic cars and kit cars. Apparently, this carpet only went into a few Cobras." he noted the lack of any smart-ass reply and continued: "I hope you can see, this narrows our search down to people who have some connection with one of just a handful of cars. That's going to be quite a varied demographic so we'll be able to eliminate a fairly large percentage from our investigation based on what we know about the attacker; all the women, of course … though then again, in this day and age maybe a few of the women can't be ruled out!"

Richard didn't miss his chance.

"But surely, Detective Chief Inspector," the dead-pan delivery was rich with sarcasm, "you'll be able to balance those numbers by ignoring gays and some of the more effeminate men?"

Logan had vaguely intended his out-of-character comment as some sort of comic relief; instead he realised it portrayed him as less resistant to Richard's goading than he would have liked to be. A glance at Claire revealed she was probably with her husband on this one. That sort of laddish bawdiness had never come naturally to him and was utterly misplaced here. It was the sort of thing he should have kept for the guys at the station, or better said, should have kept if he had ever been one of the lads. As he tried to read Claire's expression, the way the blue of her eyes seemed to have iced over, he felt himself reddening. "Oh, I didn't mean…"

"Maybe not a topic for flippancy, detective," interjected Richard. "The person…man who attacked my wife is still out there."

"My apologies, Mrs Treloggan, for that last remark."

Round and round, even faster, went the signet ring while Richard stared at him and Claire held her silence. "So, is that everything?" asked the former.

It was a chance to get back on firm ground. "Mr Treloggan, the point is we could be looking at concentrating our search on as few as twenty households. If that isn't a cause for excitement – a breakthrough – then I don't know what is."

"No, you probably don't." No sooner did he make his facetious statement, than Richard went quiet. Perhaps he couldn't quite believe that with such simplicity the case might at last be moving in the direction of resolution. There was something else in his eyes – hard to define, but it looked like a moment's uncertainty.

"Wonderful, Inspector Logan." It was Claire. She looked down at her hands, which were clenched in front of her. "Perhaps we'll be able to put this thing behind us soon."

How did she mean that? As Claire looked at both men in turn, Logan realised she might not even have known the answer herself. Was it the curse of women that an innocent comment could be so easily misunderstood; that men looked for complexity where sometimes there was none to be found?

Then Richard crossed the room and put an arm around his wife. Logan wanted to believe it was a shallow territorial gesture, but as far as he could see it was a move of genuine affection. To his shame, he felt a flutter of despair as Claire leaned into the embrace. He averted his eyes, taking in the disordered rows of bottles of booze in the cabinet. The silence started to weigh on him so he shrugged it away: "Well, having given you that hopeful news, I'll leave you alone now and be back in touch when we have further developments. We won't rest until we have him…the perpetrator." He hesitated. "Thank you for your time." One look at Claire told him she was still swimming around in cloudy depths, trying to keep her feet away from whatever had been stirred in the mud at the bottom.

"I'll see you out," said Richard. For once, there was concilia-tion in his tone.

Logan addressed his last words to Claire. "You know, it's such a pity you can't remember more about the attack."

Just the way she lifted her head to respond spoke volumes. "The pity is, Detective Chief Inspector, that I can remember that evening at all."

With a silent curse to the gods that made him so clueless in her presence, he gave the slightest of nods and left.

****

Strange things happen. As the door shut – in the words of the old maxim – another one opened and, later that night, Claire and Richard had sex for the first time in over a year. Also, unbeknownst to them, they achieved a rare moment of togetherness during the act, as each considered how lucky it was the other couldn't read minds.

4

Earlier that day

"So they've stopped now; the nightmares."

She closed her eyes and nodded. "Yes." Freddy reached over and put his hand on hers; not a gesture he could have made, even with his dear friend, if this had been a formal session.

"I'm glad for you."

"Not as glad as me," she opened her eyes again, "but thank you. It was like going through the whole thing again...every night."

"I thought you said you could never remember the details of the attack?"

She shuddered. "I can't remember the dreams either, except that I was consumed by darkness and fear, and couldn't breathe – and that much I do remember about the night in the woods, in a subliminal way." Now she looked across at him. "You still doubt me, don't you?"

"Don't be ridiculous."

"Hmmm." Her eyes narrowed. "Well believe me, this fucking amnesia is more frustrating for me than anyone else. I've been little or no use to the police."

"Well, I guess the uninterrupted sleep you're getting now makes it one-nil for the little blue pills against the little grey cells," he made a faux-theatrical gesture of exasperation. "much as it pains me to allow psychiatry its little victory." He leaned forward, growing more serious. "I want you to know, I understand why you can't come to me on a formal basis. As a clinical psychologist, who knows how long my approach might have taken; whether indeed, as a friend, my own concern would have affected my ability to bring you a psychotherapeutic solution? Those little blue pills my colleague prescribed for you with have the advantage of not being emotionally involved."

"I'm off them now; weaned myself away."

"Yes, but they've helped you close a door you'd left open. How long's it taken – just two weeks? And before that; months of hell. You're stubborn. It could have all been over that much quicker for you."

She withdrew her hand. "It will never be over."

Freddy raised his hands. "No – poorly phrased. I apologise. I just meant that sleep would have helped you."

She shook her head again. "Even those two weeks were too long to be on pills. Who knows what such strong medication back then might have done to my unborn child? I wasn't prepared to take the risk."

Freddy smiled. "How is Cissie?"

"Safe." She knew it was a peculiar response. "Although according to the examiner he didn't seem to have, well, you know…" Freddy nodded. "…if any harm had come to Cissie it would have been as if he had – to both of us…" she put her hand to her throat "…God, Freddy, does that make me sound like a very sick woman?"

He patted her arm. "Let's just say, if anything good has come of this, it's the forming of a bond between you and your child that wasn't there before." Claire felt her face flush in annoyance, but Freddy pushed on; brooking no argument. "C'mon Claire, you know you resented being pregnant; thought it meant you wouldn't be…" he parenthesised in the air, "…sexy and desirable anymore and that it would be the death of your career. But now, it's as if you were both attacked and so you have that shared experience. Cissie's more than a child to you now; she's come to symbolise your survival. Hence your decision to forego sleep and put up with a brightly lit spare bedroom rather than risk harm to the foetus, even though you couldn't stop those terrible images from projecting against your eyelids. That's not the Claire I remember from before all of this; the resentful mother-to-be." He leaned forward. "I'm not sure I like it; who am I going to moan to now about children?"

Claire grinned, resigned to losing that argument. "If there's one thing worse than a smart-arse best friend, it's a smart-arse best friend who's also a psychologist."

"More coffee?"

"I'd love some. Given how old that Nespresso machine is, it still makes a damn good Lungo."

Freddy Dessler grinned as he crossed the office and busied himself at the tray, staring at the smart town houses across the street as he spoke.

"Continuing to be a smart-arse for a moment; I'm guessing, for the months after the birth, it wasn't just the sleeping pills you were refusing; you wouldn't accept defeat." He paused for a moment, stirring the tea. "But you know, Claire, even top athletes know when to take a rest – it helps them to continue winning. You were wise to give yourself a break; taking the pills, I mean."

"I guess you're right.

"Are the police any closer to finding someone?" He looked over his shoulder and surprised her by winking. "What's Logan of the Yard got to say about it?"

Despite the circumstances Claire felt the unwanted attentions of a blush kissing her cheek. "Oh, he's hopeful; but then he always is. It's part of his job, isn't it?"

"I wouldn't say that doe-eyed look you described is written into his job description. I am very sure he's hopeful."

"And I'm not sure doe-eyed was the right description." She paused, looking for the word, but unable to nail it. She couldn't deny it; Ben Logan seemed to be perhaps a little more interested than was healthy. "That was very arrogant of me. He's remained very professional."

"Of course, as a Detective Chief Inspector should," Freddy's tone was heavily tongue-in-cheek, "but the eyes have it, Claire — whatever that mysterious *it* is."

"Whose eyes?"

No sooner said than regretted. Within the bubble of her friend's practice, his humorous approach had made her careless and she had allowed the cork to loosen for just a moment. Freddy would know now. For her, the greatest surprise had lain not in the fact of a young, eligible and high-achieving policeman finding the pregnant victim of a sexual assault attractive, inappropriate though it might have seemed to some, but in her response to it.

It seemed her body hadn't switched off its hormones after all, despite her ordeal, and that opened a very large can of worms, because Richard was probably implying the opposite to any of their closer acquaintances who would listen; immersed in his battle to win hearts and minds. In his eyes he had done all a husband could to be understanding. She believed he still loved her but, a year on, he was finding it harder to conceal his growing disappointment and frustration.

The post-traumatic amnesia had left a void; a blank canvas on which her imagination could paint with as fine or broad a brush as it pleased. So, when Richard whispered in her ear, all she heard was the disembodied voice from the back seat of her car. That she couldn't remember what the attacker had said was both terrifying and infuriating to her and a source of much frustration to the police. The mere brush of fingertips against her skin brought on panic attacks. And how was this for an ironic touch; she knew she'd not been penetrated by her attacker, but she wondered whether she would have been able to cope better with the aftermath of an actual rape. Perhaps such physical brutality might even have given Richard a greater understanding for her coldness.

Freddy brought over the coffee, having taken her sudden silence as a tacit request not to discuss further the subject of Ben Logan. "I assume my psychological profiling hasn't helped them much then?" He looked down at her. "You know, that interview was one of the toughest things I've had to do. I didn't want to get involved. If you hadn't insisted I was the only one you would trust…you were so vulnerable; damaged. All I wanted to do was put my arms around you and comfort you. Instead I had to switch off all emotion and try to give us the best chance of nailing whoever had done that to you, which meant catching you while the ordeal was still vivid." He slumped back in his chair. "I'm not sure whether I succeeded. It was no surprise your mind suppressed the things it feared would harm you. I'm confident something will trigger the memories one day."

"I look forward to it." The response was a touch petulant, but she was powerless to prevent it. Part of her admired Freddy's tendency to lose himself in his forthright, some would say tactless or slightly smug professional persona. It must have been good to have some chameleon in you.

Freddy leaned right forward again, making it impossible for her to avoid his gaze; clearly her heavy-handed sarcasm hadn't escaped him. "You must believe; I never doubted you. I know some of the police did because of your lack of detailed recall. I know they suspected it might be a cry for help and hoped my findings would suggest you were a bit flaky; making it all up. They're Neanderthals; they couldn't hope to understand the shadows lurking at the back of the cave. Although not this Logan, perhaps; he's the one who requested the profile even though he hadn't arrived here from Hampshire at the time. It would be interesting to meet him in person one day."

"Anyway," said Claire, her tone softening by way of an ersatz apology, but also keen to move on from the topic of Logan, "suppose I'd better get moving; get back to Cissie."

"Richard looking after her?"

She gave a little snort; more in resignation than derision. "No, she's with mum. He's away on business again; working harder than ever."

"Mmm." Freddy pursed his lips. "How do you feel about that?"

Claire sighed as she stood. "Oh, I suppose I can't blame him. He's got to plough his energies into something as he can't plough me."

Freddy's brows furrowed, but she could see he wasn't embarrassed. Claire and he had shared the most candid of relationships from their time at university together. Barriers tended to splinter when one of your first memories of each other was a night of uninhibited, drunken fumbling. She, on the other hand, regretted immediately the throwaway line and hurried on. "Anyway, there's a dark corner of me that hopes things don't change – I mean between Richard and me. Perhaps that's why I don't go rattling the door at the police station demanding updates." Now she stood. "Enough; I'd better get moving."

"How're you getting home?"

"Driving." He looked concerned. "It's ok. Funnily enough I never think twice about getting into the car."

"But he's still out there. I don't think it's right that Richard lets you do it…" He hesitated. "I'll rephrase that; I'm surprised he's ok with this."

She leaned across and put her hand on his cheek. "That, Freddy, is why he's married to me and you're not."

He frowned again. "I won't even bother to try to understand the metaphysics of that."

She smiled. "For somebody who's not married yet, that's probably a wise decision."

5

A positive consequence of the way his brain malfunctioned, something that he now acknowledged and recognised was almost certainly a medical condition, was an acute awareness of peripheral motion and any accompanying sound. Even if he hadn't seen, from the corner of his eye, the postgrad's suede brogues – were they still called Hush Puppies? – falter in mid-stride, he would have detected their momentary lack of movement.

Detected – an interesting choice of word. Even now, right at the beginning of his studentship, he found himself questioning the choice of forensic science as his subject and wondered whether, in the world to which he aspired, the difference was in the detection rather than the detail. On the one hand forensic scientists played a crucial role in the solving of crime. It had seemed in many ways the natural choice for him with his eye for, or perhaps better put, reliance on detail, plus his rather solitary ways. Who better to commune with than the dead? They, in turn, would not judge him – assuming he didn't fail them, of course; the innocent ones at least. But detecting – was it another word for sensing and therefore of equal appeal? When your judgments about people weren't based on their faces, and so were not distracted by them, didn't that make you the perfect communicator with

circumstance, treating every moment on its merits and immediate outcome?

It was something to think about. However, at his school they
hadn't offered 'Becoming A Detective' as a career path, being
more concerned that you didn't throw their administration and
processes into chaos by committing that cardinal sin of choosing
both sciences and arts for your A-levels.

However, just getting away from home to university had been
fine by him – for now.

During these reflections, the postgrad's shoes had moved on, as
did his attempt at conversation, conducted in what might have seemed
a tone of perfect insouciance to a less receptive ear. Perhaps it was no
accident that he chose to stand out of sight by the coffee machine for
the moment: "So why did you throw the watch into the sea?"

It was the obvious question, no less troubling and incisive for
that. "I guess out of anger and frustration."

"This may sound unsympathetic under the circumstances,
though I assure you it's not," the postgrad paused, "but anger and
frustration with what?"

"Everything. The world. Of course, I wouldn't have known
that at the time."

"So now, with the gift of hindsight…anger and frustration
with what?" The postgrad wasn't letting go.

"Naturally, I was angry that my sister was dead. She may not
have been my friend, but she was the one thing that stood between
me and loneliness. I guess I was also angry with her for being dead.
How…why had she let that happen?"

He expected an interruption at that point – a rebuke for
saying Anna had somehow been compliant in her death – and was
impressed when none came. He pushed on: "She was precocious."

"You mean precocious puberty?" asked the postgrad. "Ahead
of her age in physical development?"

He reflected and then continued: "That too, now you mention
it, so perhaps some might say I shouldn't be blaming her in any

way, but we make choices even when young. She hung out with the wrong people, dressed…" Was he pushing his luck? He decided to moderate his words. "…perhaps inappropriately. None of it mattered; standing on that clifftop I knew I would get the blame in some way. I knew I wouldn't be able, despite everything, to tell my father his golden girl had been a bit of a…had indulged herself ahead of schedule."

"You know that for sure?"

"Death and taxes are not the only certainties." Whether a light went on in the postgrad's eyes, he couldn't tell, but the practised stillness of the listener's body revealed he got the allusion. "Sometimes you have to go with what your instincts tell you. Perhaps that's what happened to me when I threw the watch into the sea."

"Still, it's a pretty damning indictment of your sister."

"Well, if I could see it at twelve years old, it must have been true. Don't get me wrong; I'm not condoning what happened to her, it's just that she put herself in a position where it could happen."

He took a sip of the coffee; noted the way his host did the same, presumably an attempt to bond with his guest by mirroring his body language. How often had he done that himself, hoping to compensate for not being able to read people? How often had he failed? It was a question he could not answer.

"But obviously you were also angry with the guy who had done this to her, so why did you throw away what might have been a key piece of evidence?"

He looked out of the window, considering for a moment. "I wish I had a definitive answer for you. Perhaps I felt time should disappear into the sea with her – but that's a bit poetic and unlikely." Now he turned back to his host. "I don't know – you tell me."

The postgrad parted his tented fingers and raised his hands in semi-defeat. "Would that I knew. Maybe you just wanted it all to go away at that moment."

"Perhaps – I think there's an element of truth in that, in some surreal way, but as time's gone on I think I've come to believe I had another much darker motivation."

The postgrad leaned back in his seat, crossed his legs and flicked his black fringe away from his forehead. "Okay, I'm all ears."

"I think I knew somehow, even then, that the guy would get away; that my inability to point a finger and say with certainty *'That's him'* would lead where it did in fact lead. You have to remember, I was a misfit hiding in plain sight. I knew even then I had a condition that set me apart from others and I was trying to mask it. I was young; I didn't want to be different."

"But the watch might have changed that. You might have solved a crime and been someone; the hero"

"I saw it differently. If I had handed it over to the police and they found the owner…if I had then stood in front of him and still not been able to say he was the killer…"

"That's hardly a dark motivation in a boy; not wanting to appear stupid."

"Well here's where the darkness comes in." He took a moment, seeking the right words. "Maybe at that moment I just didn't want it solved."

The postgrad's legs uncrossed once more, elbows again resting on knees. Perhaps that was why so many academics had those leather patches on their jackets. He peered out again from beneath his fringe. "Go on."

"I lived in the shadow of my sister. With her out of the way, perhaps I could at last emerge into the daylight. Was I just glad she was gone?"

Again, to his credit, the postgrad said nothing. No morality lecture ensued; no talk of the abhorrence of jealousy and the like. He seemed a man who could be trusted; a man to be called on in one's hour of need.

It was certainly time to move on.

"Whatever I might have been thinking, what I suspected would happen happened. Anna's body washed up, cleansed of its sins, and likewise my Purgatory began; and while in the minds of others she became this innocent victim, I grew to hate her."

"Okay – that's strong; unsettling." The postgrad stood; walked across to the window and stared out as he continued: "I applaud you for being so truthful. Why did you hate her?"

"For all the reasons mentioned before and a load of new ones." He reached for his coffee, found the cup was already empty. "I saw the impact of her death on my mother."

The postgrad turned from the window. "And your father presumably."

"Yes, but that involved a different set of rules. My mother's grief was the pure, unadulterated despair of someone who has borne a child. For my father, posterity had lost a princess, Jane Austen, Mother Teresa and Marie Curie rolled into one." The cup started to spin in his fingers and he poked a finger through the delicate china handle to prevent it. "I believe those words, that disembodied voice, emanating from behind me at the police station marked possibly the last time he spoke to me with any inflection, never mind affection. He just shut off from me. They both did, to an extent, though a mother can never completely close the gate." He paused, eyes squeezing tight for a moment. "Her decline – a broken heart and subsequent alcoholism – are part of why I hated my sister. Then there was the loneliness on birthdays; Christmas. The 'X' on the gift tag hardly constituted love." He looked out of the window towards an abstract concept of home. "It's my intention never to go back. Spiritually I left home a long time ago. I think I might even change my name; a complete fresh start" Now he looked around the office. "What I see here, these battered books, photos and quirky mementos, are the cargo of a life's journey, rather than the jetsam. Before I left home, I emptied my room of almost everything in it."

"You're not a guy who does things by halves, are you?"

"I'll rebuild my life. The stuff they gave me, it means nothing. None of it was wrapped in love or gift-tagged with a hug. In fact, it made me start to see material things in a new way. I felt my parents' gifts were poisoned by the emptiness of the gesture." He sat up straight. "You know, now I think back, I remember washing my hands scrupulously one time after I had a vivid recollection of throwing the watch away, as if my life has been forever contaminated by the deed, the whole filthy history that watch had witnessed.

"We – my parents and I – spent less and less quality time together; no tea by the fire or TV dinners. You could say presents replaced presence. I doubt they ever had any inkling about my condition, such as it is. They never questioned why everything in my room had to be in a particular place. Once, years before, my mother took me to the doctor because I had a little facial tic. He said *'he'll grow out of it'* and so I did. I suspect my mother still believes that rule applies to life in general.

"Despite all that, seeing her distress broke my heart. You start questioning whether it is worth caring about somebody that much – I mean her feelings for my sister.

"My life became – has become – lonelier because locally I started to be seen as the guy who couldn't identify his sister's murderer, despite having looked him full in the face. Even the couple of close friends I had put distance between us.

"And then the other rumours started."

"And they were?"

That no-one else had seen this guy; that it was known I didn't get on with my sister; that she'd been heard telling me to get lost down a side-street by some other pupils; that I had run home and said she'd been pushed over the edge of a cliff – by someone else."

It felt as if hundreds of thoughts hatched and squirmed in the room. At last one of them found voice through the postgrad, fingers almost welded together to give nothing away. "Forgive me this, but you know the next question."

He looked into his host's eyes and noted they were a striking blue. "Are we legally under terms of doctor patient confidentiality?"

A regretful shake of the head. "I'm afraid not."

"Well then you know the next answer."

The postgrad took a breath as if to start speaking, but his visitor moved on.

"There was – is – a dark corner of my soul that accepts why my sister met her fate."

"I believe that's a well-trodden path."

"I'm not just talking about whether she was pushed off a cliff. The French have the *crime passionnel* – I understand that." For the first time he felt some anger towards the postgrad, but allowed it to subside. "Sex is as much of a destroyer as love. It's very easy to blame a man's primitive urges, or a woman's, but all of us have a duty to recognise that destructiveness. It would be easy to argue that my sister didn't understand what she was doing, but she did. I saw it more than once; how she could smash open the thin, almost translucent shell that separates man from beast; the more fragile it was, the more she seemed to enjoy wielding the hammer. But it destroys the destroyer too – sex – and there's collateral damage. Just as it killed her, so it ruined others; not only because of what she'd done, but what it led another man – and then me – to do."

6

The disorientation which had marked most of Claire's life since the attack was as nothing compared to the dizzying news of the arrest of Jack Geddis.

When the police brought him in, on the instructions of DCI Logan, for questioning as the owner of a Cobra fitted with the specialist type of carpet matching the fibres found at the crime scene he confessed to the attack rather too readily for some officers' liking, particularly Detective Inspector John Heath, who had been the man in line for DCI before Logan had been brought in from outside and surprisingly promoted ahead of him. An IT consultant by trade, Geddis' only previous brush with the authorities had been a headmistress reporting seeing his car parked a few too many times near her school, given that he had no children. He had insisted at the time that he just liked to park up and work on his laptop. The police had advised him to move on. According to witnesses amongst the waiters and regulars his next preferred work-station was the café opposite the clinic, where he had spotted Claire arriving for her baby-care class and, in his words, developed an urgent, crushing need for her. Something in his mind had snapped. He had observed how she eventually left the clinic, appeared to have forgotten something and went back inside. He'd planned to break in to the car, but found it open – clearly she had failed to lock it when she nipped back inside. Then he just waited. The rest, as they say, was history. In terms of how he would have broken into the car, the set of lock jigglers found by the police search team on visiting his home said much about his capabilities on that front. As he appeared to be something of a classic car enthusiast, a picture started to form of a man who knew his way around, or into, vehicles.

The officers feared he might have the makings of a serial confessor; his lonely lifestyle – he seemed to have no real friends – and middle-of-the-road job leading him to seek a moment in the spotlight. However, he revealed too much knowledge about the details and timings of the case for them to ignore him.

Claire was both elated and exhausted by the time she found out she would not be required to give evidence at the trial in person. Part of her wanted to confront the man, but eventually she decided to take advantage of the new legislation that allowed her recorded evidence to be presented. It meant the trial was a surreal, disembodied affair, both for attacker and victim, though that in itself, in a strange way, was in keeping with Claire's featureless memories of the ordeal. She did wonder whether this might prevent her reaching closure. Her nightmares had never revealed a recognisable human face. She had to decide whether seeing him in the flesh, not just in the newspapers, and hearing his version of events would leave them branded forever on her mind, setting off her night-torments again, or would help transform him from satanic to sick and sad. She went with the former, though not before stopping to wonder whether the faceless shadow of her dreams might just return, more potent than before.

Both she and Richard were outraged when a combination of Geddis' previous blameless life, a plea bargain and the fact that he had not committed a penetrative act of rape meant he stood to get out of jail, in the event of parole, in less than five years, given the charge of indecent assault on a woman carried a sentence of ten years. Claire's lack of recall left her lawyer with little leverage; the latter had wanted to go for the charge of abduction of a woman by force, which carried a sentence of fourteen years.

****

When it was all done, Logan paid one last visit – at least in an official capacity. It was late afternoon, and again he was acutely aware of the tension, but this time, sad to say, not between the Treloggans; it emanated from him. Richard appeared to have just returned from work and was looking smart and handsome in a Boss suit, with his receding hair slicked back in a way that gave him an air of authority. Then there was the bottle of wine this married couple was sharing.

"I'm not wearing my work hat this time – guess you'd call that a helmet." Logan smiled in apology at his own joke. The signet ring orbited his finger and he added a little tug at the tip of his tie. "Well, that's not strictly true; I do want you to know that, if there's ever anything more I can do, in a professional capacity -" he glanced at Claire and cursed himself in silence for doing so, hating the power she held, "- to help you recover from this ordeal, you mustn't hesitate to contact me."

When Claire looked at him he saw pain in her eyes and cursed his inability to translate it. Was he more damaged than he knew for hoping it might be sadness? Who wished that on anyone? "Thank you, Inspector. Thanks for all you've done."

He took his courage in both hands. "Unofficially, I wanted to invite the two of you out for a drink, or perhaps a meal, to celebrate."

He could have damned himself to hell for that last, poor-ly-chosen word. It was her effect on him; precision seemed to desert him in her presence. How ironic – if only she knew what a difference that could make to his life! She had the grace to cast her eyes down.

"Inspector Logan," said Richard, "thank you for the offer, but I think I speak for my wife as well when I say that we'd like to put this behind us now. It's not really cause for celebration, just a big relief. We're both very tired."

Claire looked up again, but for now, for Logan, the dimly-lit space which her soul inhabited seemed closed off to him. "I'm sorry, Inspector; perhaps another time?"

He hoped his nod of understanding was convincing; that his eyes hid the resentment he felt at the bottle of wine in such non-celebratory times.

God, he wanted her! Of all the impulses he fought to control, this one appeared to be beyond him. Perhaps in some ways it was as well then that, unbelievable though it seemed, the time had come to walk out of her life, despite all his unfounded hopes and every way he had tried to make them less so. He had done his job too well. There remained no single thread that bound him to her. How was that for an irony, when just a few threads of fibre had nailed Jack Geddis and brought closure – with every nuance that word possessed? Case over. Nothing left to do but reflect on and regret all those times he'd had her alone and failed to make her see that they trod the same demon-haunted paths. Instead here he stood, staring at their rather old-fashioned décor and fittings, wanting nothing so much as to rip their quaint world apart; ruin it, so that it stood smouldering and he could rescue her. Because none of this – their rustic-chic, soft-furnished world of comforts and conveniences – should have survived the earthquake of a year and a half before. The after-shocks alone should have been enough to leave their marriage as rubble.

Now a rather more prosaic thought surfaced; a desire to smash his fist into the suave face of Richard Treloggan, for having the arrogance to believe that someone like Claire, someone damaged, could ever love him again. After all, what was love; just the shroud in which you buried desire and obsession?

They were looking at him; unreadable in features but not in thoughts.

"I understand entirely," said Ben Logan with a practised smile. He turned, then turned again and reached into his jacket pocket. "Here." Crossing the room, he removed a card from his wallet. This he handed to Richard between the tips of two fingers, a gun-like gesture lost on the man blocking the road to his dreams. "In case you lost the first one or, as I say, if you ever need anything."

His second attempt to leave was also interrupted as he reached for the door handle.

"Ben…" it was Claire, who had risen from her chair and stooped where Logan had been standing to pick up something from the floor, possibly his heart, which seemed to have plunged through him at the sound of his name on her lips, "…I think you dropped this." She was holding a key towards him.

"Thank you." He took it. Did her fingers rest a second longer than necessary in his palm? Perhaps not. "Sorry. Must have fallen out of my wallet. It's my spare door-key."

Richard Treloggan's gaze had turned towards Claire when she had used "Ben" and now he was watching Logan; did that suggest maybe he thought there had been some ulterior motive in dropping the key?

In a perverse way he was grateful at that moment for the strained atmosphere; it made it just a little easier to turn and walk out of their lives.

For now.

7

Richard Treloggan certainly did not have a clue he was being watched as he slipped into the café for lunch. With more than four years having passed since the arrest of Jack Geddis, perhaps he had grown careless.

The watcher could guess how these things ran; how the risk intensified the thrill until you were no longer satisfied with the humble fumble in a hotel; then having got away with it a few times, feeling you would never be caught, your partner returned unwell a few hours early from work to find you in a position you wouldn't want to have to explain to the divorce courts.

It can only have been such misplaced confidence, which led Richard to choose a local diner for a tryst; worse – a window seat. Was he trying inverse psychology? *Of course I'm not having an affair. Do you really think I would be so stupid as to shit on my own doorstep and in full view…blah, blah, blah?* But the hands touching across the table; now that was arrogance. He was going to get what he deserved and would deserve everything he got, as far as the watcher was concerned. Looking at the 'Greasy Spoon' Richard had chosen for this liaison, here was a classic case of going out for burgers when you had steak at home.

The watcher smiled, not without a hint of malice, and whispered: "Say cheese."

Through the opening in the magnolia bush came the sound of a camera shutter slicing chunks of time; a devilishly sharp knife, leaving life in pieces.

This changed everything.

8

As he approached and looked up at the big iron gates, the strength of his simmering resentment took him by surprise. She seemed to have allowed these fortifications to shut off her heart, an ability he envied. Beyond them he could hear the crash of the Atlantic raging

Four and a half years. Was it really that long since he had last seen her? He relished the prospect of the look on her face when she found him on her doorstep; the discomfort it might cause her.

Indeed, a reminder of what she looked like would be quite something in itself! Strange to think he might have wandered past her any number of times in recent years and not known. He moved on quickly from that thought, given its implication that she may have chosen to avoid him. The fact remained; his memories of her would have been entirely visceral if he hadn't looked through the case file before making this visit.

Wondering how she was doing was pointless, not only because he was about to find out, but because he had, already, a gut feeling that she was strong. Like all women she would never forget her ordeal, but unlike some she would forge on, driven by the combined forces of an innate maternal love for a child he suspected she had never adored and her will to survive the worst men could do. He should have admired her, not harboured this sense of rancour for her having failed to call on him in the nearly forty thousand hours which had passed since the case had closed and he'd had to walk away. It would seem weird to most people that he'd calculated that rough figure on his drive over, but somehow the phrase "*four and a half years*" hadn't adequately captured the passage of time. Nor had there been any other case in the interim immersive enough to deaden the passing of those hours. It seemed North Cornwall's coastline was as wild and angry as anything got down here.

As she answered the gate's intercom her choice of words told him everything he needed to know, as did the pause that preceded it; a seeming eternity packed into perhaps two or three seconds.

"DCI Logan."

So, it seemed, she was putting up further barriers of formality straight away.

Looking towards the camera, he raised both hands in mock apology. "The very same."

She buzzed him in rather than telling him to buzz off, which he supposed was a positive. As she opened the door her face stirred no jolt of recognition in him. That at least wasn't her doing; prosopagnosia rendered all faces equal on first, and indeed all subsequent, encounters.

"I didn't pull rank to handle this enquiry, I swear to you. I was at the station when the call came in and thought you might welcome a familiar face." Oh, the irony of that statement!

"I believe you." Did she? A shaky exhalation of breath accompanied her smile. "Come in." He would have loved to believe the slight quiver in her voice was a result of her finding him at her door. Unfortunate, then, that the circumstances surrounding his visit, rather than the fact of it, suggested otherwise.

If he hadn't already known it was her, then her little tug on the hem of the turtle-neck sweater, a style she favoured, confirmed it, as well as revealing a figure that still matched his memories. She gestured towards the stairs and lowered her voice. "Cissie is having a sleep upstairs so we'll have to keep our voices down."

He was taken aback; disappointed too, if he was honest. "Oh – it's not half-term, is it?"

"No, but I've pulled her from school for a couple of days." She responded to his enquiring look. "It's tied in with why you're here…well, kind of…"

It felt peculiar walking in – a stranger who had once been a protagonist in her life, just as she was still in his fantasies. His resentment was growing – for the hold she exerted over him even now. For having given no hint that it was mutual. For not having heard a word in the intervening years – even prisoners got letters from home. For the fact that everything about her led him to forget he was a copper; a good one. He clung onto that last thought as he entered. He would need that remove, that objectivity, more than ever in dealing with this latest issue.

If there was any exhilaration, which after all would have been inappropriate under the circumstances, it was tainted by anxiety. His thoughts sickened him – a flash image of her auburn hair fanned out across a white sheet beneath him. Though he squeezed his eyes tight the picture was on slow-fade – or was he just reluctant to let it go; a vision of what could never be? He needed to break the cycle.

"Are you okay?"

Silence greeted his question, so he turned.

"I'm sorry, DCI Logan?" She looked as if she'd had to jump-start herself. Was that a hopeful sign, or a bad one? Her continued use of his formal title was certainly the latter.

"I asked if you were okay," he continued, "but I think the question's answered itself."

She shook her head. "I'm not really sure how I'm doing."

To his ears, trained to compensate for the failings of his visual memory, there was dissonance in her voice. Her eyes were fixed on him, but their gaze was enigmatic. He held that gaze and noticed how, after a few seconds that were clearly more uncomfortable for her than him, she folded her arms; the classic defensive gesture.

This was confusing. He'd expected to find her in one of several possible moods when he heard about her call to the station, but this particular anxiety had not been on the list.

"Do you need to…" he hesitated, "…see anybody; talk this through?"

She gave what might have been a stoic smile and gestured for him to sit. "No, but a good friend of mine is a psychologist, should I feel the need."

"Oh yes," Logan made a repeated clicking motion with his fingers, "Freddy…Freddy Dessler; that's it. That was a detailed profile he did for us. You insisted it was him or no-one."

But I could be that good friend; your best friend.

He pushed on. "I'm a bit old-fashioned in that sense; first I put my faith in forensics."

"Strange – he said you requested the profile."

Claire's arms remained folded, but by tilting her hips, she seemed to adopt a more challenging posture. It emphasised the other detail he'd taken in when she had answered the door; her hair had a leonine quality to it now, her previous more layered style having apparently been abandoned in favour of, well, abandonment.

He needed to refocus. "Indeed; pressure from above meant I had to. As I say, for me, no matter how hard a criminal tries there's always something that will catch him or her out. We've almost reached a point where it's impossible not to leave a trace of yourself at the scene of a crime – that's what got our man in the end. But in conjunction with science, I have another process. My next port of call is…" He hesitated, distracted by a fragment of memory as he remembered sitting at a murder scene in Winchester, allowing his mind to absorb the place. "Well, I'm not sure what to call it. I was going to say instinct, but it's something more than that. It's kind of…immersing yourself in the crime scene, almost as if its ghosts might lead you somewhere. There was this case…" He was rambling. "It doesn't matter."

As if a switch had flicked off.

"Go on," prompted Claire. However, his focus had changed and he looked at her.

"Really, it's not important."

Claire returned his gaze, said nothing. There was something odd about her silences, but without them he believed she might prove even harder to read. "Would you like a coffee?" she ventured at last.

He considered for a moment. "Yes, that would be nice."

"Come through into the kitchen."

That he had never been invited through into that part of the house before hung in the air between them, till it was replaced by the steam from the kettle. It made him feel better, that abstract moment of sharing; the steam in turn replaced by the scent of Kenco; a homely aroma – deceptive, as it turned out.

"So, are you back at work, Claire?" He didn't know whether being familiar with her was appropriate, but he felt comfortable enough with it and ploughed on.

"I've been doing some work for my old company." She was stirring the coffee, perhaps with too much intent, and her gaze seemed to fix on some distant point beyond the brick wall of the kitchen. "I'm not fooled; they couldn't just get rid of me, but I'm out of the loop. It's mainly keeping a few of the least-interesting accounts turning over, that sort of thing, and a bit of other consultancy-type project management." She stopped stirring and brought the cups over. "I'm fine with it. I get paid and to be honest, since the whole business, I'm not sure what I want. Richard's more than happy that I'm home-based."

They sat opposite each other at a table of distressed wood, appropriately enough, and Logan produced his notebook – times and technology moved on, came and went, but the ubiquitous police notebook remained. As he opened it, Claire pursed her lips and gave an approving little nod. "You have nice writing. Very neat."

He looked up, and then down at the pad in atavistic panic. No matter what she saw, his mind's eye couldn't help but be drawn almost every time to a particular tell-tale page, long since removed from an older book. For once, mild obsessive behaviour had little to do with his discomfort. It was his mark of Cain; evidence suppressed to further his career whilst meting out his own form of justice.

She was looking at him, this time puzzled just by his silence. "Oh, well, it's important not to get things muddled up." He gestured with the pad. "These often form a part of your testimony in a courtroom. Can't afford to give the defence a loophole."

Logan drew a careful line under the last entry, wrote the date and looked at Claire. "When did Mr Treloggan disappear...or rather, when did you last see him?"

"I last saw Richard two days ago." There was that discord again in her voice.

Logan frowned. Something was jarring. "And you've only just raised the alarm?"

"You know how it was...is with him, Ben."

It was as if, sensing her initial response sounded defensive and chameleon-like, she had changed its hue simply with the use of his Christian name. He knew she saw it in his eyes; the effect on him, hearing it from her lips in that intimate setting – she might as well have just placed those lips on his spine directly. His need for her was laid bare and he couldn't be sure yet whether it excited her or elicited pity. Still, his detective's senses remained alert enough to recognise that she wanted him onside.

She continued: "It's not unusual for him to be a little the worse for wear after a business meeting and not get around to calling me – for one evening. But when the second night came and went..."

"Okay, so you've not heard from him for forty-eight hours?"

"No."

"Have you spoken with his colleagues?"

"I called the office shortly before I called you. They were vague.

The cynic in me wondered whether that was their default response to any married partner contacting the office and Richard definitely preferred me to stay out of his working life. But the bottom line is, they don't know where he might be."

"You used the past tense."

"I'm sorry?"

"You said preferred." He took a moment's pleasure from that, but the observation was valid. He moved on. "Does he have a diary?"

"He's old-fashioned enough to keep an A4 one on his desk and he transfers stuff from there onto his phone calendar, but I've looked in there and there's nothing obvious, which…"

"…makes it even stranger." Logan completed her sentence. "His passport?"

"Always keeps it in his briefcase just in case."

Claire rested her elbows on the table and plunged her fingers through her auburn hair, while Logan sought to remain focussed. He'd always assumed that mannerism of hers to be innocent in its wantonness, but she had him unbalanced right now and he was reassessing many things. Again, through the silence and the open window, he became aware of the waves, out of sight and hundreds of feet below, but still raging in a battle against stone that they were destined to win, while seagulls screeched their demonic cries.

"We'll have to find out the number and check all the ports and airports." He hesitated for a moment while Claire looked out of the window. "Pardon me for asking, but how had things been since the trial?"

She turned back to him, knowing why he'd asked, but seeming to resent the question.

"Do you mean emotionally or…?"

He raised his palms. "Whichever you want to talk about."

"Supposing I don't want to talk about any of it…but if you want to know whether we're fucked or have been fucking, it's more the latter. Does that answer your question?"

He said nothing; saw no sign that she regretted her abruptness and wondered just who she had become in the last four and a half years, forty thousand hours, whatever. Yet what else had he expected? He gathered his thoughts and moved on:

"And continuing in this spirit of openness," – she couldn't help but give a tight grin at his riposte – "do you know whether he was – sorry, is – having an affair?" His casual error with past tense was nothing of the kind. Rather, he needed to understand; why did she already appear to be washing that man right out of her auburn hair?

"No, but I wouldn't blame him."

"I would."

So much for pulling himself together. He felt a blush surfacing and knew his weakness gave her added strength.

"Have you married since we last met, Ben?"

"No." The reply was instantaneous and landed like a glass marble on the table between them, rolling down the imperfections of its surface till it dropped with a thud in Claire's lap.

"Do yourself a favour – avoid that vale of tears like the plague."

Much as it ripped at his heart to admit it, being here again brought home to Logan why his departure from the scene had, in all probability, not come a moment too soon. It was obvious he carried a torch for her and that could have had only negative implications for a senior police officer dealing with a woman who was the victim of a sexual assault. Yet her previous question and the deliberate intimacy of using his first name – he was sure it was loaded. Though he might be damned for thinking it, he wondered if she had tried as hard as she might to discourage him during that original investigation; if not, did that mean she shared culpability? Like before, the discomfort and embarrassment in his eyes when she caught him looking could have been merely a reflection of hers, albeit a distorted one. How complex was the human beast, which lay awake at night squeezing its eyes shut against flying shards of memories – images of invasive hands in intimate places – yet took almost wilful pleasure in imagining strange fingertips touching its skin? She owed it to both of them to keep a distance. He recognised that now.

Perhaps with this in mind, she continued:

"It's been a slow process – reviving a comatose marriage; an imperfect, incomplete one. But we'd made progress. Knowing that animal Geddis was behind bars helped. You cannot know, even if you think you can, how grateful I am to you for that."

That last line, and the soft tone in which it was delivered threw him off kilter. She should have been a police officer; good cop, bad cop – she could have played either.

She continued: "Despite the absence of passion, or maybe because of it, I'd learnt to relax into…I guess you'd call it an unspoken truce; a.k.a. our sex-life. I'd even climaxed a couple of times."

God, why did she insist on hurting him by sharing such an intimate detail. Because he was Everyman?

"I could tell he assumed I was faking. But I wasn't. Both of us backed away from discussing it, as if the truce might shatter. What did it matter? What do you think, Ben; does it matter?" She paused. "Sorry; too much information, I guess."

On reflection, he'd misread things entirely. This was not a woman trying to keep a distance; but for the moment, her true purpose remained as much a mystery to him as her husband's disappearance. He needed to take back some control. "I wouldn't know. What I do see is that you've slipped back into the past tense again. In your mind, is the marriage over, or is it simply that you fear the worst?"

Claire got up, opened a drawer and pulled out a packet of cigarettes. She gestured with it. "Do you mind?"

"No." Logan frowned. "I didn't realise you…"

"I gave up when I discovered I was pregnant."

He gestured upwards with his eyes. "And having a young child doesn't bother you?"

"You might want to rephrase that question." She lit up, exhaled shakily and then pursed her lips. "I guess that sounds a bit harsh."

"A bit."

"I don't smoke when she's with me, but right now she's recharging her juvenile batteries upstairs. I do love her…but I'm not a natural." She drew on the cigarette and examined the glowing tip. "I suppose this cancer stick is all the evidence you might need for that, Detective Chief Inspector."

He tried smiling, but the smoking was bothering him. He caught himself starting to fold one of the pages of his notebook and with an effort of will intertwined his fingers. Having seen that, as always, she observed his discomfort, it spoke volumes that she refused to put out the cigarette, whether it made him uncomfortable or not; perhaps because it did. Maybe she guessed, too, that his irritation was in part due to her having kept her smoking from him; a guilty secret she'd not shared.

Now he delivered himself a mental slap across the face. Time to get a grip. "At least it's stopped your hands from shaking." Touché. Like many a high-ranking officer, he hadn't got there just by withholding evidence. Nor had the comment been merely an attempt to score points. For as long as he had been involved in the case, he had never known Claire's hands to be anything other than steady, even at her lowest ebb. In one thing during this day's interchange she had been consistent – that slightest of tremors where before there was none.

She wasn't letting the ground shift that easily.

"Back to your original question, Ben. Four years ago, I might not have blamed Richard for having an affair. Funnily enough, that possibility was the first conclusion I jumped to, around the time his usual…" she paused, seeking the right word while drawing deeply on the cigarette, "…perfunctory, antiseptic love-making became a bit more frantic and urgent. He started ploughing me with greater intensity."

He saw she was enjoying this now. It was giving her a sense of power, knowing these images were both torturing him and strengthening his need for her. What it said about her need for him was another matter – and immaterial. Something had changed.

She had changed. Surely forty-eight hours without her flawed husband hadn't prompted this.

She continued. "I'd started to sense the presence of a third party in our bed; a sort of ghostly ménage-a-trois. But when you've spent some unwanted time in the company of a true pervert, a few harmless thoughts about ersatz lovers are nothing, as long as you don't cry out the wrong name in the heat of the moment. Besides, didn't I have my own library of images to draw from?" She looked long at him. "Don't we all? There's almost comfort in them." She paused. "But not anymore."

Claire came to the table again, bringing her ashtray with her; knowing her last words had left an unspoken question hanging in the air. He wasn't about to ask it.

Now she leaned forward and moved on:

"Look, to an outsider – no, to my mind as well – I know the situation contains some of the classic ingredients for an eternal triangle; the emotionally fragile wife; the successful husband who travels extensively and probably finds no shortage of lovely shoulders to lean on as he declares that his wife doesn't understand him." She leaned back. "I doubt whether references to my assault would play any part in Richard's seduction techniques. Far better the floozies think his frigid wife is simply denying him his conjugal rights, which of course they're only too willing to provide. If I were a policeman, that's what I would assume; he's missing in combat, so to speak. To be honest, it's exactly what I *was* thinking when I called."

"Mummy, mummy!"

Both of them frowned and turned towards the kitchen door at the sound of the voice from upstairs. For one of them, at least, there was concern as well as irritation.

"Mummy!" The girl sounded distressed.

"Oh no," said Claire, stubbing out the remains of the cigarette. "What's the matter?"

"Strangely, since Richard left this last time she's been having nightmares, which has never been the case before. Work that one out." She looked at him in apology. "Would you mind seeing yourself out?"

"Sure thing." He reached into his pocket and produced a card. "In case you've lost the old one. I'll let you know what we find."

He wondered whether she could tell he was both reluctant and relieved to go.

As Ben Logan left, Claire wondered whether he had any idea just how hard it was not to scream after him to stay.

9

"From what I can piece together, it's always set in this idyllic scene; a waterfall plunging over cliffs, with emerald green downs stretching from snow-capped mountains all the way to the cliff edge. I leave her bedroom window open, so maybe somehow the sound of the sea is registering. There's a fairy-tale castle in the mountains – a bit like Neuschwanstein, I guess – and oblique sunlight, but I haven't been able to work out if it's rising or setting. Some details vary, or she forgets them the longer she's awake; sometimes there's birdsong, or wild horses galloping across the downs. She seems to be standing watching all this from a window. And then it starts; there's a blot, or at least something dark appearing over the cliffs, and from what I can tell – remember, she's just five and a bit so it's really hard for me to piece together – it's throwing a lengthening shadow, so it must be approaching. The worst part is, whatever this thing is, it's saying her name; whispering it over and over: *"Cissie; Cissie."* She insists that's what it's saying." She looked up from the swirling darkness of the coffee mug. "That's when she wakes up, usually in a sweat; always crying."

She looked at Freddy, who said nothing for a time while he digested not just what he'd heard, but what he was seeing. From the reappearance of dark circles under Claire's eyes – her bruised beauty – one would have been forgiven for thinking she was the one having the nightmares. Then again, if her little girl was waking in the wee hours, it followed that the mother's nights were being disturbed too. And of course, she was worried about her husband – to an extent; Freddy wasn't blind to the tenuousness of the threads that bound the married couple. Yet he was sure that something else was affecting Claire, as if she had awoken to find she was made of flawed glass, which the merest of taps could shatter. Maybe Cissie's nightmares had reminded her of the horrors she'd endured, night after night, following her own ordeal.

It seemed she had read his mind, because her next words pre-empted his question.

"I know what you're thinking; I'm looking too deeply into things because of my own experiences and Cissie's missing her father, pure and simple."

Freddy looked at her. "Are *you*?" Perhaps he shouldn't have said it, but it was out.

She glared back at him. "That's neither fair nor relevant. I'm not here to talk about me."

"Are you sure?"

"What on earth do you mean?"

Freddy put down his coffee mug and, even though he felt comfortable sitting that way, resisted the temptation to fold his arms, aware of the defensive signal it gave out. "Okay, I'll spell it out. Richard's been missing for four weeks. Your daughter's having recurrent nightmares, during which someone barely visible is whispering her name, ergo someone who knows her. It's always an idyllic scene, but with an ominous shadow – or is it hope? – just out of sight over the cliffs. In the meantime, you might be repressing a need, in whatever form it takes, for the officer assigned to both cases who has reappeared; fighting against it because it was a man who has left you feeling unclean and somehow guilty. Are we here to analyse Cissie's nightmare, which seems to be nothing more than a psychological trauma brought on by the stress of her father's absence, or to assuage your feelings of guilt?"

Claire put down her mug with a bang and placed her hands on the arms of the chair, ready to lever herself up.

"How dare you!"

Freddy remained motionless; not a muscle twitched. "Good to see the old, feisty Claire is still there. You're not paying for this abuse, so why not sit down and take it?" The slightest of grins pulled at the corner of his mouth and Claire did indeed sit down with a thump. Then she laughed, but it was an uneasy sound that spooked him with its message that this wasn't the old Claire after all, but a new, rather twitchy one that was trying too hard.

"You're good" she said, "wrong, but good."

"Wrong about what? Those tendrils of lust spreading through your body? My advice would be 'Give it up'." Her eyes threw barbs at him and he spread his hands in faux arrogance. "You missed your chance to keep me, so the only way is down. Better to have loved and lost than never…" He trailed off, left the attempt at humour when he saw the slight curl of Claire's lips. "Hey, I'm sorry."

It hadn't been the best choice of quotes under the circumstances of Richard's disappearance. Still, it didn't warrant the latent anger confronting him now, which took him aback. The gleam in Claire's eyes hadn't faded away; it still lurked in there, a slow-dying ember glowing red in the night, waiting for the breeze which had extinguished his bravado to bring it to life again. This was new; discomforting. Men had a lot to answer for; that was for sure; Claire had always been a passionate, ambitious, but well-balanced soul before. He decided to push on.

"Don't despise yourself, Claire. None of us can predict our responses to the various stimuli around us. You can't help feeling drawn towards Ben Logan; he was there to support you and Richard at a bad time, and now another trauma has come round, it's only natural you'll lean on him. And I doubt if Cissie's pretending to hear her father's voice to try to make you feel guilty about it. She's too young to be that cunning."

"But surely just hearing a man's voice is enough to remind her Richard's not there. Ben's been round a handful of times to check on me...us." Claire stopped; pulled a face that suggested she was reconsidering something. "Or at least that's what he says. Each time, within a few minutes of his arrival, Cissie has started calling for me, distressed. I certainly agree that she's not that cunning – you know, trying to stop Ben having any ideas – so is hearing a deeper male voice perhaps affecting her?" Freddy stayed silent; there was no definitive answer to that one. "I wish it were as simple as you suggested, Freddy, but just to put you straight; firstly, I don't even know what – if anything – I feel for Ben Logan; secondly, there's been nothing physical; and thirdly, how do you explain the fact that Cissie's nightmares started the very day Richard disappeared? He'd been away for several nights at a time before and...never a whimper."

Freddy put his tented fingers to his lips. "Mmm... that is interesting. Maybe this is the first time she's been old enough for it to overwhelm her cognitively. Does she recognise the voice?"

"No, it whispers. It's sinister; she says it's 'scary'."

There was perhaps half a minute of silence, and then Freddy said: "Look, I don't believe in coincidence. That's why I'm sure Richard's disappearance and the commencement of the nightmares are linked. I do believe very strongly in the effects of stress on the subliminal brain and all the demons who ride in its slipstream; cortisol, sleeplessness, hypervigilance. So, I'm going to suggest hypnosis."

"What, on a five old?"

"The very best – a young mind unfettered by prejudice and corruption; uncluttered by the jetsam of growing older and not always wiser. If we can find the trigger, maybe we can fire the silver bullet."

Claire shook a head full of misgivings. "I don't know, Freddy; hypnosis. What if things go wrong? Is it even legal? What if you can't bring her back from...wherever you send her?"

He gave a light laugh. "Claire, you've been watching too many stage shows or Hollywood films. Look, if she had been much younger then I might have baulked, but actually children are great at relaxing their bodies and their minds. All I'll be doing is…well, think of it like this; I'll be washing the windows so she can see more clearly. Or would you rather she wakes up in a cold sweat each night, screaming, while some vague monstrous shape lurks outside? What are you scared we'll find, Claire? What if we find nothing? Does that scare you even more?"

"Lay off a bit, will you, Freddy?"

"Sorry." She looked uncomfortable. In his professional excitement he had not taken due care of her finer feelings. Reaching out and putting a hand on her arm, he said: "Look, we may even find that she's got some psychic link to Richard and that she can lead us to him."

"Oh, don't be ridiculous." She folded her arms, the movement designed to shake off his hand. As body language went it was pretty unambiguous and rather surprising.

Freddy saw the slow burn of anger and fear reignite in her eyes. If he could have laid his hands on Jack Geddis at that moment, he'd have ripped the pervert's head from his shoulders for having poisoned Claire's soul. Nevertheless, what she needed now was a rock in the midst of the storm, so he held firm. And he had just remembered something, which as well as being common ground, was genuinely exciting under the circumstances.

"Claire, do you remember that game Richard played with Cissie, where he held the toy bumble bee behind his back?"

There was a moment's silence, then a grudging "Yes" directed more at the window than at him. Unfazed, Freddy continued:

"Remember how many times she would point to the correct side to find which hand he was hiding it in?" Claire's mouth relaxed a little, becoming less tight-lipped – just for a moment – as the warm blanket of a memory enclosed her. Then her lower lip trembled. Freddy knew he had her attention. "On one occasion, I started to count; twenty-seven times she made the correct choice before we all collapsed laughing. I told you I don't believe in coincidence."

Claire was still looking towards the window, but she'd started to shake a little. She tried to disguise it, but it found expression in her question. "Freddy, do you think a psychic link can survive beyond the grave?"

The tears came.

****

"She's under."

"So quickly?"

"I told you yesterday; an uncluttered mind."

"I didn't know hypnosis was one of your branches of study," she whispered, still staring at the composed face of her daughter before putting her hands to her own. "God, what have I consented to?"

"Don't worry – oh…and there's no need to keep your voice down," he said. "I've shut out everything extraneous for the moment. Yes, I studied it in the hope of using it to bring women under my spell!" One look at Claire showed his joke hadn't even registered, which was, on reflection, probably just as well. "Okay, let's get started. Her name will be the trigger."

He turned his full attention to the little tot in pigtails and dungarees decorated with unicorns, sitting with her eyes closed in a chair that dwarfed her. She had gone under with such ease that for a moment he had felt like God. Freddy crouched down in front of her, even though he knew she couldn't see him.

"Hi Cissie, can you hear me?"

"Yes."

"Do you know me?"

"Yes, you're Freddy; you're not *him*."

"Not who, Cissie?"

"The other man; mummy's other friend. You're her nice friend. She hides the other friend."

Freddy shot a glance at Claire that said *"No feelings for Ben Logan, heh? Nothing physical happening."* She spun away and went to the window, while he turned his attention back to the little girl.

"That's right, I'm Freddy. Do you know where you are?"

"I'm nowhere." The girl's quiescent voice, issuing from an almost inanimate face, gave the bald statement a sinister air, as did the fact that her words had lost the curly edges of childishness.

"Nowhere?" He frowned. "Describe nowhere."

"Nowhere has a big window." Freddy looked at Claire and she gestured towards the window in front of her with a shrug of the shoulders.

"What can you see through the window, Cissie?"

"There's a big field. The sun is shining. There's water splashing and butterflies and horses. Nowhere is nice, but..." She stopped.

Claire had left the window and returned with caution across the room. This sounded like a typical setting for one of her daughter's nightmares and she wanted to be by her side. However, the girl had seemed calm – no reason she shouldn't be, given the pleasant setting – until that last note of doubt.

"Yes, 'Nowhere' sounds very nice, Cissie," said Freddy. He was astonished that, not only had she gone under with such ease, she had arrived in the world of her dreams as if it were always beneath her feet, just waiting for her to miss her footing. "So, what is it you don't like?"

Claire tensed; went to put her hand on Cissie's shoulder, but Freddy discouraged her.

"Well..." The little girl hesitated. *"It's* coming. It always comes."

"What is it, Cissie?"

"I don't know."

"Then how do you know you don't like it?"

"I don't like its voice. It whispers. It's coming over cliffs to get me and I can see a shadow."

"Everyone has a shadow, Cissie." Then a thought struck Freddy. "Where's the sun?"

The girl paused as if checking; pointed behind her.

Mmm, thought Freddy, that made the shadow even more interesting.

"What's it saying, Cissie?"

"I don't know."

Claire and Freddy exchanged glances.

"Are you sure? Is it your name?"

"I thought so, but no."

Claire went to speak but stopped herself.

"Try to hear it, Cissie"

A frown puckered the flawless skin of the little girl's forehead, and then she opened her mouth. "I don't understand it."

"What is it?"

"Nice sneezy." Her mouth took on an incongruous shape as she tried to catch the timbre and intonation of the shadow-voice. It made Freddy's skin crawl. "Nice sneezy."

The hypnosis session might have continued if Claire hadn't collapsed to the floor with a thump.

10

"Hey…hey…you okay?"

She heard his voice, felt his hand on her cheek, but her eyes hadn't opened yet. When they did, there was to be no gentle reawakening; she burst to the surface like someone escaping from a submerged car and Freddy had to hold her arms to stop her reeling from the couch back to the floor. She fought him, gasping.

"Ssshhhh, ssshhhh, she's asleep, she's asleep" urged Freddy's sibilant whispers, caught between concern for his friend and not wanting to wake Cissie. "I brought her out of hypnosis and into a state of suspension; didn't want to leave her at the mercy of the dreams from Nowhere."

At last the face of her friend came into focus above the drowning pool into which Claire had sunk. She stopped thrashing. When he released her, she became aware of the pain at the back of her head and put her hand there, wincing as her fingertips touched a lump.

"You fell heavily when you passed out," he said. "You okay?"

She took in her surroundings, saw her little girl asleep on the chair, and then felt faint again as other things started to rise from the black waters beneath her. Slowly they came, dislodged from the silt and tangling weeds where they had lain waiting. One of them was recognisable – the figure of a man, bringing the past with him as he reached towards her, or rather…

…he lifts his hand in front of his eyes as he approaches the car and tries to block the light from the beams.

She finds herself noting irrelevant details; the multi-coloured pinstripe of his charcoal grey business suit; the tiny motif above the breast pocket of his pale blue shirt and the immaculate fold in the knot of the red silk tie – murder's looking smart today. She checks the central locking again, but otherwise remains paralysed.

Yet there's nothing like an unexpected voice from the back seat of your car to shock you into movement – from your bladder if nothing else – while the touch of the sharp point against the back of her neck is almost feather-like. The disembodied voice stage-whispers:

"Nice 'n' easy – tell him I'm your husband. Tell him I'm sleeping in the back because I feel ill. Do it, or you'll never see that child you're carrying – and your knight in shining Beamer won't ever see his family again. Not a false word or move, or I swear he'll get it, and so will you. Don't try looking round at me, or let him engage me in conversation – I promise you, it will be the last thing you do." *The blade is pressed harder to emphasise the point in all senses. She reaches for the window button.* "It's down far enough; don't wind it any further; you wouldn't do that if you thought he was an attacker, would you? Besides, we wouldn't want him smelling what I can smell – give you a fright, did I?" *She hears him settle in the seat again.* "Remember… nice 'n' easy."

The suit is at the window and stoops to look in. She tries to calm her breathing.

"What do you want? Why have you been chasing me?"

She sees a friendly face; middle-aged, with grey hair and features that register only concern.

"I think someone got into the back of your car," *he says, trying to sound authoritative, she presumes for the benefit of any unwanted passenger who might be contemplating violence.*

She weighs it up. The suit looks like he keeps himself fit enough, but she knows nothing about the intruder and there's an ominous remembrance of Freddy's words in the void; psychopaths often have the strength of several men. Plus he has a knife. But Claire has watched so many films where victims have gone without a fight to their desperate, bleak deaths; where it seemed worth resisting and, if necessary, dying on their own terms, rather than cowering in terror before a madman whose intention never was to show mercy. She wants to weep in frustration at her indecision. She should take her chances, shouldn't she? Okay, the suit is slightly blocking the door, but she's sure he'd spring back. Her body prepares itself for the leap to freedom — and that's when it registers; she's wearing her seatbelt. In her panic it could cost her vital seconds as she fumbles with the fastening.

She freezes.

As if he's read her mind.

There's a slight increase in pressure between her breasts and she realises that her tormentor has hold of the seatbelt near the lock. He's given it the slightest of pulls; a gentle reminder.

"I'm sorry? Yes…I mean no…it's my husband. He's not hiding, just not feeling very well, so he decided to lie down in the back. What made you think…?"

It takes all her self-control not to release the welling sob that's building in her chest. Meanwhile, the man glances towards the back seat, but if he has doubts he seems to keep them to himself. "I was parked just along from you in the pay and display. I was on the phone and just before you arrived I thought I saw the car door shut, but I really wasn't sure because I wasn't looking properly. Then, when you got in and didn't turn to communicate with anything or anyone, I was going to come over, but you drove off in more of a hurry than I expected. I don't know — I just had a bad thought in my mind and wouldn't have forgiven myself if I'd heard later in the press or somewhere that something had happened. You sure you're okay?"

"Yes." *Please God, let her smile be unconvincing and the suit rip open the back door to drag out the monster. Except she's locked it.* "It's fine, really."

The man smiles. "In that case I'm sorry I scared you. You can't be too careful, can you?"

"Thank you for your concern."

With that he returns to his car and hope disappears down the road; a pair of red devil's eyes tormenting her as the rear lights fade into the darkness.

The pressure on her breasts increases, though this time it comes from a pair of hands, which pull her back against the seat. A voice whispers; the words carry almost physical force, invading her senses. There's something else about that voice now; distortion and a slight muffling. God, he sounds like he's wearing a mask! She assumes he must have removed it when her would-be rescuer was approaching.

"Well done. Now, before we go any further, give me your phone."

"I don't…"

"Give me the fuckin' phone!"

She knows it's pointless pretending and his demand is all the more sinister for being whispered, so hands over her mobile. His next words are uttered with such playfulness, they make her feel sick: "Okay, let's go have some fun."

****

"Turn left here. Nice 'n' easy does it; it's a narrow lane – a lonely place." Impossible though it seems, the hoarse stage whisper makes the whole nightmare worse.

They pass signs saying: DANGER – KEEP OUT. She wants to say something; try to communicate with him and humanise their relationship so that he would have more of a problem harming her – stuff she's heard Freddy referencing regarding a case in which he became involved – though the first time she tries to speak when they resume their journey the knife is pressed against her neck and he tells her to shut up.

"Don't worry about those signs," he hisses – his voice never rises above that hideous whisper. "This leads to an old quarry; they're going to be redeveloping here and want to keep people out. There's no danger – in a manner of speaking." He laughs. If the sound were guttural she might cope better, but it maintains a matiness so out of keeping with the situation that again she feels bile rising in her throat. "Now make sure you concentrate on your driving. We've got a couple of miles to go and I certainly won't be paying attention to the road."

With that, his left arm snakes around the seat. He's already made her remove her coat before they set off and now he starts to unbutton her blouse with surprising dexterity. She tries not to look at the hand, perhaps because the sickening sight might tempt her to bite him, which could lead to all manner of reprisals; or maybe because she wants to detach herself from what's happening.

The blouse now open, he pulls her bra up roughly, freeing her breasts. He cups one, kneading and squeezing it, keeping his head to the right of her, so she can't see him in the rear-view mirror, though all the while his stertorous breathing is in her ear. She can't help but look reflexively at the hand now.

"Watch the road, bitch."

Far worse than his laboured breathing is the sound of a zipper opening. The pawing at her breast becomes more frantic; likewise the ragged, rasping groans he's starting to emit. There's a sudden gasp, a pause, and then a final tight squeeze on her breast before he releases his hold. She feels him slump back. The bile resumes its upward journey, burning the back of her throat as she imagines, despite her best efforts, his semen staining the seat. Claire tries to take hope from this. Perhaps now the full act of rape won't happen. Plus, he must have left his DNA in the car.

Too soon though, the full-on fear returns. Why are they driving to a quarry if masturbation was all he had in mind?

The mind – it feels as if hers has already been penetrated and defiled.

Once more he crushes her unspoken hopes that anything might be over. "Whooh!" That sickening jollity is there again. "I just wanted to get that one out of the way, so I can be more composed; enjoy what's to come."

****

The silence is the worst of it now, or rather the lack of any communication. She has become almost impervious to the cold and assumes, with remarkable detachment, that she must be in some sort of shock. Likewise, she has grown used to the smell of the sack over her head. But she misses a human voice – even his – as if words would somehow give her a point of reference in her helplessness; proof that she is still alive; that the universe has not just abandoned her.

The evening itself, though, remains far from quiet. A capricious, but angry wind buffets the trees, by turns whistling through the lifeless branches or rattling them in a danse macabre. And now imagined whispers try to fill the void; taunting her with talk of the violent penetration to come; perhaps even a shallow grave here in the woods and another missing person. And the person that will never be – the one in her womb.

She has no idea how long she's been here, but it seems an eternity since she heard her captor's footsteps or voice. Strange how that is not the comfort it might have been.

Her only hope lies in him being a watcher. He had made her park the car in front of an old Portakabin, which might once have been a site office, put a sack over her head and then led her into the woods. Then he had ordered her remove all her clothes – slowly; almost a striptease. Forcing her to lie down naked on her front, he had bound her wrists and ankles with what felt like cable ties, and then made her kneel. After that – he disappeared, leaving her shivering with an ague of terror that by far overrode the November winds.

At last it had occurred to her that she might just have been abandoned after all, but as she made an attempt to struggle with her bonds a voice by her ear made her shriek and she stopped.

Now she wonders whether she has slept, impossible though it seems, because the approach of death suddenly wakes her; hurried footsteps from several feet away that stop in front of her. She cringes. Once more his hands fumble with her breasts. There's the breathing again, like in the car, followed by another groan, inches from her ear.

Then the feet move round behind her and, despite the cold, the blade of the knife is icy as it rests on her shoulder. His mouth is by her ear once more.

"Thank you – and goodbye."

Her bowels open.

She hears the zing of the blade, as it slices through the plastic ties around her wrists and ankles, and collapses face down in the mud.

The sound of an engine brings her round again. It's fading. He has gone. Taken the car. He can have it. God, she's alive! She's more than happy with the exchange.

It takes time to open the intricate knot holding the sack, but she bursts from its smothering coarseness into the darkness of the woods and the cold night air, blessed wonders of creation that they are. Then on cramped, trembling legs she staggers in what she believes is the general direction in which the car headed.

Somehow, she finds her way to the weed-overgrown car park in front of the Portakabin. A battered, barely-legible sign reveals that this was once part of Trelawney Tile and Brick. The office is unlocked and the tap in the bathroom still works; there is even a handful of paper towels left in the dispenser — better than most public toilets, she thinks, surprised by the appearance of a gallows humour she never knew she possessed. She might almost be tempted to believe someone up there likes her, if it weren't for the little matter of a sexual assault. She manages to wash away the worst of all the different types of filth, her need to be clean far outweighing the chill of the icy water against her skin.

And now all she wants is to be home. He has taken her clothes, for whatever perverted reason, and the November cold combined with delayed shock brings her muscles out in further spasms of shivering. She realises there is no chance of making it back to the main road without risk of hypothermia and hunts through the buckled metal cupboards in the vain hope of finding something to wear. Now she reflects on just how much one's priorities and perspective can change, when she rejoices at finding a battered high-vis jacket. Soon its grubby nylon is preserving the remaining vestiges of her body heat and its crusty fleece lining might be the comfort of cashmere against her skin. There are a few pairs of worn-out work-boots and she pulls on the least large pair — none of them are small — still several sizes too big for her.

Claire is even able to smile when she puts the handset of a bulky, clay-stained telephone to her ear to be met by silence. That would really have been one for those who believe in guardian angels, if she'd found a live line. This ruin of an office has provided a temporary sanctuary, but she has to think about stepping out into the strengthening wind that is shaking these flimsy, abandoned walls.

Although she knew nothing of the existence of this quarry before, Claire has a rough idea where she is, though not how far she has to go. Her feet are numb by the time she finds her way from the disused office back to the forest road. What drives her on is the primal will to survive. Then there is the need to protect the unborn child; evidence of a maternal instinct that, rather like the dark humour sustaining her this night, she hadn't realised was part of her make-up. Added to the mix is the faint, but undying spark of joy at being alive and this carries her to the main road. It says much about the remoteness of that road, that no other car passes her as she staggers on aching, freezing legs for a couple of miles till the lane hits the road that leads home. The toecaps of the work-boots rip at her feet, but she reminds herself of the hell that this trek would have been on bare feet and soldiers on.

At last, the gates of the home that she has, from time to time, viewed as her prison come into view and never has she been more grateful to see them. She prays that Richard is back as she presses the buzzer; her strength is all but gone. The intercom crackles into life — a wonderful sound. She knows her face is visible on the security screen, but given how she must look, perhaps his question is no surprise: "Who is it?"

Between answering that question and her speaking again, about an hour passes. She has no recollection of it, nor, it seems, of anything prior to leaving town. For now, that brings more relief than panic. The hot spray of the power shower is a misty curtain through which she steps into a world of post-traumatic amnesia.

****

"My God!" Freddy had gone pale.

She didn't know what to say now. It had been like listening to another person.

Freddy continued. "The words — they triggered it, didn't they? Those words — *nice and easy* — or 'nice sneezy' as Cissie called it. They were the key to everything your brain had locked away in a padded, soundproof room!" She looked at him, quite lost. "And your nightmares; all along they've been the muffled sounds of that imprisoned monster throwing itself against the walls. There's never been that detail – ever. Your brain chose to blank it all out – a survival mechanism. All you ever told us was that you'd been subjected to an ordeal." Freddy gazed into nothingness. "There was none of the finer detail. For heaven's sake, we didn't even know you'd been followed. And whoever that other driver was, the guy in the suit, he wouldn't have stepped forward as a witness, because he didn't know he was one. As far as he was concerned, you were a woman whose husband was feeling sick."

He sat back with a slump, but Claire stayed perched on the edge of the couch where she had sat immobile since starting to tell the tale – as still as an Egyptian deity staring across the desert wastes with profound, blank eyes. Freddy made to get up, but then had second thoughts. After a moment's hesitation, during which he weighed up whether she would want a man's arms around her right now, he came over and placed a tentative hand on her shoulder. She leaned into his embrace and he hugged her. He saw there were no tears, and had to ask: "How do you feel now?"

"I don't know. I'm not sure whether that will prove to be cathartic or disastrous."

Then, perhaps because years of friendship had put them on the same wavelength, they exchanged a look of comprehension and dread, before turning slowly towards Cissie, still asleep in the big chair. This session had raised more questions than it answered. What on earth did she know about that horrible event? More important, how did she know?

Now Freddy spoke in a hushed tone, no longer so confident that his words weren't penetrating the induced sleep. "Well, we know the attacker hasn't spoken to her directly; he's firmly behind bars." Then he sprang up "Wait a minute!" ...before reconsidering. "No – no, it couldn't be."

"What?" said Claire.

"There hasn't been enough research about this topic."

"C'mon, spit it out, Freddy. I'm open here." To her friend, she seemed anything but.

"Well, you know how they say unborn children may be receptive already in the womb to outside stimuli, such as music? I wonder if…"

"No, Freddy. Don't go there." Claire raised her hands as if fending off someone's unwanted attentions.

"But Claire, it was a major trauma. And those nightmares – you wouldn't take the sleeping tablets because you were scared they would harm Cissie. It's just possible that your agonies transmitted to her."

Claire had gone pale, her eyes scanning around her in distraction, yet seeming to search for something specific. Then Freddy slapped his forehead in frustration and said:

"Ach! I'm such an idiot. Haven't I just said we've never had the details before? Your nightmares were vague and frightening, not carbon copies of the event. So how the hell would Cissie know about the phrase '*nice and easy*' anyway?"

"So where does that leave us?"

He slumped onto another chair, but shifted around in agitation. "I don't know. But it does make it less likely that the menacing shadow whispering to her is Jack Geddis."

"Why?"

"Research suggests – and it *is* only a suggestion – that any stimuli need to be repetitive to affect the embryo. A specific, one-off phrase or event would be unlikely to provoke a response."

"But what if it was playing through my mind every night in my dreams? Just because I couldn't remember the details doesn't mean they weren't there."

"I don't think so. My experience of dreams is that they're symbiotic in origin and symbolic by nature; you know, teeth falling out, that sort of thing. I doubt Jack Geddis is wandering around in them in person."

"Well who the fuck is it then, if not him? Who's put that phrase into my child's head? And try to speak English."

Freddy was stung, but held any retort in check, even though he was just trying to help. This new Claire – the one with dry tinder for a soul, just waiting for a spark of anger to ignite it – scared him a little. However, given the revelations of the last few minutes, he could understand the anger; he really could.

"I don't know." He leaned forward in his chair. "But it's certainly…" He stopped himself in time; his professional self had been about to say 'exciting', "…a conundrum. The thing that puzzles me is the timing," he continued, frowning.

"What do you mean?" Again that flintiness, as if Claire didn't have the time for his musings. He guessed she needed a cure rather than a diagnosis.

"Well, these things normally require a trigger." He paused for thought. "Claire, as you haven't mentioned nightmares before, I assume Cissie wasn't prone to them."

Claire shook her head. "No more than any other child."

"But ever since Richard disappeared it's been every night?"

"I've told you this already. We're going over old ground here." She looked at the floor, chewing her lip, only half paying attention. "And while I agree with the fact that something strange is happening, I can't accept that Richard's disappearance is anything more than coincidence."

Freddy scrabbled around for a suitable image and then said: "Well, try to think of the brain as a bottle of fizzy drink. Latent within it are the ingredients for quite a volatile reaction. Most of the time it sits there inert; the odd bubble rising to the surface. Then someone shakes the bottle." He looked at Claire. "If Richard's disappearance hasn't shaken the bottle, you tell me what has."

She looked past him out of the window then back to the floor. "I don't know."

"What if unbeknownst to you Richard took his leave of Cissie the morning he left? You said he went very early, before you were up. If she was tired and a bit emotional about him going away again, it might have upset her equilibrium. She loved…" he raised his hands in apology, "…sorry, loves him unconditionally, like any young child." He kept his hands raised as if to ward off the dart of a look she threw at him. "Hey, I'm only examining the possibilities. And that scenario might be enough to traumatize a young girl. Or what if…" He stopped all of a sudden and scratched his ear with rather too much intent.

"What?"

He hesitated, but it was no good. Claire might have been edgier these days, but she still knew him too well for him to get away with hiding something.

"What if something bad *has* happened to Richard?" He stopped as he saw the pain in her eyes, though its tint was faint enough that he believed he could carry on. "Let's hope not, because God knows you have enough to deal with. But…what if Cissie does have a psychic channel open – and it's her father who's calling her?"

"What – using a would-be rapist's words?" She laughed; a joyless sound. "I think you're barking up the wrong tree, Freddy. Sure, she misses him – more than I do, may heaven forgive me – but she still thinks he's away on a long trip."

Claire looked across at the little girl; still asleep, but in the light of that afternoon's events, who knew what she was absorbing?

Freddy shrugged. "Well then, maybe by coincidence she heard something on the day he left that frightened her and has released all these negative energies. It's just a shame something didn't shake your bottle *before* the court case. All the information that's just spilled from you – all those memories – might have seen the guy put away for longer."

"Well I certainly don't regret having forgotten all that detail for the past…" Claire's head jerked up. "…wait a minute! How long did Geddis get in the end? It meant he could be out in just five years, didn't it?"

"That's what I'm saying; he got ten years, in part because of your lack of recall, but the plea bargain and his lack of previous meant a likely release on parole after five. He denied having hurt you; he denied having any sort of a weapon on him; and the fact was you couldn't prove anything to the contrary. He admitted wanting to frighten you. There were none of the typical signs of any sexual assault."

"Five years! For what that bastard put me through?"

"I agree, Claire, but you have to remember…or rather you couldn't. You went into some sort of post-traumatic shock. The fibres merely put him near your car – though without his confession they might not have been enough evidence. He admitted forcing you to drive him around and I'm astonished he admitted fondling your breasts as there was no evidence. I suspect Logan himself might have indulged in a little firm fondling of the guy's testicles in the interrogation room to get that in writing. There were no traces of semen on you – even if there might have been, you've now told me you washed yourself down – and of course he torched the car. But as all you could remember was the voice in your car and then standing in your shower, it wasn't the most difficult job in the world for the defence to get him off lightly. Amnesia's a terrible thing."

"Not as bad as remembering." Her eyes were dark, but that icy flame of anger still guttered in their depths.

"Or remembering too late." Freddy sprang from his chair and crossed to the window in frustration. "Christ, they even said the ligature marks proved nothing; said they could have been self-inflicted or the result of some sexual practice indulged in at home."

Claire spoke, and when Freddy turned, her eyes revealed only hurt and vulnerability.

"He might be out already. They wouldn't parole him without letting me know, would they?"

"I doubt that, but he was in custody for six months prior to the trial, so he could be inside for just four and a half years. But I'll check it for you with Logan." He gave her a meaningful look. "Or perhaps you'd like to check it with him yourself." He regretted saying it, but couldn't hold it back. When she didn't respond he came and sat down opposite her again. He could almost taste her discomfort. "Yes, what was all that *mummy's other friend...I'm not allowed to see the other friend*? Strange, isn't it, how the eyes of children see things exactly as they are?"

"Well in this case they've seen wrong." Defensive didn't begin to describe Claire's tone.

"Have they?" It was a retort; Freddy wasn't smiling.

"None of your business." Claire tried forcing her shoulders to relax, telling herself it wasn't Freddy with whom she should be getting angry. "And no, we haven't. My husband's only missing." She tutted in self-reproach. "What do I mean *only*? Look, it's just a maternal thing, I guess; protecting her from things she doesn't need to know. Maybe it's not just her I'm protecting." She ran her hands through her hair. Freddy wondered whether she knew how that gesture affected a man. Seeing her do it from across the Students' Union bar years ago, the first time he'd set eyes on her, had caused him to lose focus completely – a bit like now as her words reeled him back in.

"I don't know," she sighed. "Maybe I don't want him getting close to Cissie; getting his feet under the table."

There was a deep pause. "OK, back to the matter in hand," said Freddy. He hated to admit it, but the thought of her and Logan making the beast with two backs wasn't easy to deal with for a man who had known Claire since university and had only in recent years come to terms with being *just good friends*. Getting away from that topic was perhaps wiser. "If my assumptions are correct – a big *if* – we're in boggy if not foggy territory and must tread carefully. We mustn't leap to any conclusions. Is Cissie responding to her father's disappearance?" He saw Claire's lips purse with the now-familiar annoyance and raised his hands defensively. "We can't rule out anything. Or is she linked in somehow to your trauma six years ago? Does she have psychic abilities? Is this reaction or prediction? All we do know is that, in her nightmares something bad is just over the horizon and it's heading her way."

"As usual, in your excitement at the intellectual inferences, you're forgetting one thing," said Claire, the irritation scarcely concealed. "Never mind the dream world; the point I was making just now, which you seem to have missed, is that in the real world something wicked is leaving jail soon and he might well be heading my way."

11

He was kidding himself if he believed respect was holding him back. She would only have to utter the right words – and as far as Ben Logan was concerned, those words would be *Cissie, go back to bed.*

Yet perhaps those anguished cries from the bedroom, or the top of the stairs, were a blessing; a shield behind which he could hide as soon as any mood of potential intimacy was developing. Opportunity could be terrifying and intimidating. A dark corner of his soul understood what might drive a man to acts of anonymous depravity. A very dark corner. The longer the road, the wilder the imaginings – and Logan's journey had lasted an eternity, though the edge of that cliff where it had started drew him back time and again.

Of course the issue of Richard Treloggan's fate did not help matters. Logan had dismissed any feelings of guilt, a task made easier by Richard's obvious disdain for him, but the missing husband might as well have been standing in the corner; a figure from a horror comic, clothes hanging in rags on a sinewy body, one eye peering out from a lidless socket and a bony finger pointing, accusing Claire of betrayal if she gave her admirer any encouragement. In truth, and unprofessional though it was, Logan would have settled for finding the guy in that condition now, just not in the corner of the room. He reckoned Claire would deal with it too, after a suitable show of distress.

All of which contributed to his racing pulse as he approached her front door this evening. It wasn't often that being the bearer of bad tidings might just signal a breakthrough. The information he was bringing – well, perhaps it was a game-changer. Claire might just find herself in need of that rock.

She opened the door to him, the sum of her features adding up so clearly to exhaustion that even he couldn't fail to see it – and, somehow, she was all the lovelier for it.

"Come in." She pushed her hair back from her face; that mannerism which always aroused him. They exchanged awkward glances as he walked past her into the lounge; for once he could read the signals, as the way she then dropped her gaze mirrored him. As he turned, he saw her eyes flicker towards the top of the stairs; that tell-tale sign. As usual he stood like a teenager, feeling breathless.

"Would you like a drink?"

"Why not? I'm not on duty." An awkward silence followed, which he felt the need to fill. "I had a call from your friend Freddy." She looked over her shoulder at him while still trying to pour the drink, but her hand was shaking and the decanter rattled against the glass. That tinkling bell was sounding a warning; one he did his best to ignore, despite having heard it at least once before in his life. "He wanted to know…"

"Sit down…Ben."

Her marketing and PR background shone through in the use of his name, but he was aware now it was her tactic and an attempt to have him onside after her interruption, which had been brusque; more so than she intended. He remembered her use of his title and surname when he had reappeared to take on this latest case; she had kept the distance her silence of four years had helped her to build. Nevertheless, though she might have been easy to read in one way, her motivations remained damned difficult – as if his blindness for all things facial didn't make life hard enough! Was she a manipulator, or just being blown from wave to wave, terrified and insecure?

None of it made her any less compelling to him

She brought over his glass and he continued.

"Well, I can confirm Geddis will be out in three weeks."

Claire held her glass steady in both hands and stared into the distance. "Three weeks. And then his punishment is over." Her voice was sweet to his ears, but that couldn't mask the bitterness. "I wish I could be clear of the memory that quickly. I wish I could shower away the filth, instead of having the stench of it hanging around me for the rest of my life."

Logan frowned. "The memory? I thought that had been the one and only side-benefit of the shock; amnesia."

She looked at him. "Well, if you hadn't called me this evening, I'd have called you. I suspect, no matter what reason he gave for calling you, Freddy wanted you over here so I could tell you. The strangest thing happened today."

****

He was stunned. "If only we'd known." He shook his head. "Six years!"

She looked so vulnerable, staring out through the window at a world which had stopped being kind to her all those years before. He wanted to put his arms around her; would have liked to believe his motives were purely protective at that moment, but in true, perverse fashion his mind drifted back to that first meeting with her, when he had almost empathized with the attacker; when he'd struck a match way down in the basement where he stored the detritus of his sometimes-troubled mind and seen what was there. So he decided to sit where he was – for the time being.

But something else stirred in the murk; the policeman in him resurfaced, but not the avuncular bobby on the beat; rather the ambitious copper who knew how to get results by whatever means.

"Claire, I could make your problem...disappear, once he's on the outside."

Her gaze returned from that distant place beyond her window and fixed on him. He couldn't interpret the look in her eye, but could have sworn he saw there the reflection of his own guttering match-flame.

"Meaning?"

"Probably better you don't know. There are ways."

"What would that make me?" she asked.

"Safe."

He had hoped his strong, monosyllabic response would reassure her. Instead, it seemed to induce a peculiar moment of abstraction, as if it had landed in a lake years before, back when the fog of amnesia was both a blessing and a curse, and she was only now seeing the ripples.

"Maybe," she shrugged, "or an accessory to a crime – or am I interpreting your comments incorrectly? Then surely instead of being unable to deal with what happened to me I'd just be unable to live with myself." There was a pregnant silence, filled with the need for reassurances that couldn't be given. She sought them nonetheless. "Why would you do that for me?"

He hesitated. "Because I...care about you... about justice."

"And is this something any woman can count on who's under your protection?"

There was ambiguity in the question, but any encouragement she offered was overridden for him at that moment by the images and ghosts her words had stirred. Never mind a stone; she couldn't know the size of the rock she had just hurled into the still-turbulent waters of his past.

"Ben?"

At the sound of his name he trod his way slowly back. "Let's just say, no matter what some might think, justice doesn't always have to be seen to be done." He gave a little smile at his own word-play. "The system often leaves loose ends. Some people can live with that, but as you've possibly already worked out, loose ends are not my forte."

She altered tack slightly. "You haven't commented on the strangeness of the dreams."

Logan chewed on his lip for a moment, considering. "I don't have an opinion really. I believe in the here and now. I've learned in the course of my career that sometimes there are coincidences which, for whatever lucky reason, put you on the right track. Sure, there have been so-called psychics who've helped with enquiries – I don't understand it and I don't pretend to."

"Mummy, mummy!"

He managed to suppress any outward signs of irritation. *What a surprise*. He was sure the girl watched from her bedroom window and whenever she saw his car – and yes, perhaps he had called by a few more times than was professionally ethical – played the night-mare hand. Daddy's little girl. The problem was, where exactly did mummy stand? She hadn't discouraged him.

Now he realised the signet ring was twirling away on his finger. That sort of tic might have been irremediable, but today he had decided he would start turning other things around. Situations he could control. He hadn't got to DCI in such haste to then repent at leisure. He had long subscribed to the old 'no problems just oppor-tunities' adage. Geddis' imminent release had created exactly that. It was a challenge and a chance.

He gestured with his thumb towards the door. "Talking of psychic links, I'm sure your Cissie doesn't want me here. I can understand that – I'm not her father." He rose to go, a calculated risk, and was gratified to see a shadow of consternation cross Claire's features. She, too, stood as if barring his path.

"Don't be daft, Ben. It's just that she's been through a lot."

"It's fine." He hoped magnanimity came through in his tone. "Like I say, her father's away; strange guy turns up pestering her mother. You go and take care of her; I'll see myself out."

He felt a hand on his arm. Looking down he noticed that the lacquer was chipped on three of the nails.

"Ben." The couple of seconds that passed as they looked at each other contained several eternities and a number of alternative futures. "You'll come back, won't you?"

He shrugged. "I don't know. We'll certainly set a watch on your door once he's out."

"I didn't mean that."

"Let go." She dropped her hand and he smiled at the misunderstanding. "And I didn't mean that."

The girl's voice carried down the stairs again.

Before he knew it Claire was in his arms; mouth hungry; tongue, like the serpent in the Garden of Eden, promising knowledge. She pulled away from him, managing to look both ashamed and unrepentant. How he wanted her to tell him to wait there.

"I'm sorry, Ben; what I'm doing – it isn't fair; on any of us."

"I could protect you both." It was out and he wished it wasn't. *Slow down*, he told himself.

"Mummy, mummy!"

He knew she felt caught – sucked in; knew only too well how that felt. Both of them were grasping for something, anything, before they were swept away by it all, or perhaps before it passed them by.

It wasn't a time to leave questions unasked. "When you said it wasn't fair on any of us, did you include Richard?"

"No." She reddened.

"Mummy, please come quickly!"

Logan wondered for a moment what would happen if he ran up the stairs and twisted the girl's neck till it snapped. The image shocked him. It passed in a flash, but so did the shock.

Claire reached up and snatched a kiss. "But for Cissie's sake he has to come into the equation somewhere. Ben, be patient with me."

The depth of his sudden shame shocked him. "I'm sorry. After all you've been through…"

She blinked her understanding. "Did my kiss feel like I couldn't cope?" She gave a little wave, smiled and headed for the stairs.

Logan's smile might have lasted from the moment he closed the front door till he arrived home, at which point his humour always left him. However, the nature of the smile changed en route and he knew it. It was all working out to perfection.

****

At the sound of the front door closing, Claire looked in that direction and her smile didn't just fade – it vanished.

12

She's walking home across the dappled fields of a beautiful summer's evening. The only clouds in the sky are the fluffy white ones of childhood. To the left a stream is babbling; behind her the sea roars and sighs with the ebb and flow of the tide. The day is so perfect, it's a cliché. And that is the likely cause of the nagging sensation; doubt. But Nature seems to have pulled on its glad-rags to brighten her life.

Just ahead she sees her home, standing on its little piece of land, with its raised flowerbeds and swirls of lawn, which seem somehow too perfect. She's never approached it from the cliffs; didn't know you could. She'd always thought of it as private, but is it perhaps a little isolated? There's a fence and a lych-gate – picturesque or, seen from another point of view, less secure than the high electronic gates and brick walls at the front.

And that's when she hears the sound; a rhythmic dragging, as if someone is pulling a heavy, wet sack. It's behind her, as is the sibilant whispering. She looks down, expecting to see the bobbing of an advancing shadow, but it's not yet come that near.

Home isn't far away now, but it's taking time to get there, which she accepts in that half-conscious state of the sleeper who knows that dreams can't harm you unless they terrify you to death. Except she isn't sleeping, because home is definitely getting closer and she can feel the keys in her hand. They come out of her pocket in a tangled mess and the front door key has got *caught in the loop of another one. As she struggles to free it she reaches the gate and doesn't know which to deal with first; the latch or the keys.*

That's when she hears crying and looks up to see Cissie standing at her bedroom window. The little girl's hands are banging at the panes and there's terror in her eyes. What's she saying? It sounds like: "Mummy, it's coming."

Claire forces the gate open. It swings back, but she doesn't hear it clunk shut. Something stops it. The keys — the damn keys! — are still tangled and she realises that she's brought the menace right to their door. She tries to cry to Cissie — "Hide!" — but there's no sound from her constricted throat.

That's when the voice — though it's still only a whisper — explodes in her ear: "Nice 'n' easy".

****

Her eyes flew open. There was a drumming in her ears. She looked at the clock: three a.m. Her first nightmare in years — except it wasn't over. The sound of screaming from Cissie's bedroom hadn't stopped.

Claire sprang from her bed, doing her best to ignore the shakiness of her legs, and made her way to Cissie.

The girl was standing at the window. She was slapping her little palms on the panes. Claire switched on the light, thinking it was the best way to wake her daughter from the nightmare, the sound of which seemed to have worked its way into Claire's own sleep. That could be the only explanation. The girl turned, blinked a few times, but didn't run across the room and throw herself into her mother's arms as might have been expected. She seemed frozen to the spot.

Claire crossed the room and took Cissie in her arms. "I'm safe, sweetheart, and so are you. It was just a nightmare."

Cissie continued to babble into her mother's stomach as she clung to her. "It was different, mummy. The shadow wasn't coming for me."

The cold that enveloped Claire was deeper than the chill from her sweat.

"Don't worry, my darling," she said with a complete lack of conviction, "it's over for now."

"It's not over, mummy; it's getting closer."

"What is, Cissie?"

"I don't know, but it isn't nice. It was following you, mummy; the shadow."

"Who is it, Cissie?"

"I told you, mummy, I don't know. You were looking for your keys. The shadow was getting closer. It wants to hurt us. And the noise…"

"What noise?" Claire's tone was abrupt, but she couldn't help it – she was spooked.

"Swishshss! Swishshss!" The girl made a strange hissing sound and her arms mimicked pulling something.

Claire's blood was mostly ice by now.

"How did you see this, baby?" The term of endearment was more or less an afterthought. She had to force herself to remember that this was a child in need of a strong mother.

"I was at the window. You told me to hide."

Claire wasn't sure who was clinging to whom with greater urgency.

"Come and sleep with mummy tonight."

Nor was she sure who was going to derive greater comfort from sharing the bed.

The little girl nodded into her mother's stomach.

They got into bed and hugged each other tight.

"We'll stop the shadow, Cissie," said Claire. She stared at the luminous numbers of the digital clock. Green; she'd made sure this one had green numbers. The red ones on her old clock were too much like devils' eyes taunting her from the distant darkness as they faded away into the forest.

This night's events had made up her mind for her. She knew who could help her and it seemed that needed to happen sooner rather than later.

The little girl's words interrupted her musings. "Mummy, we don't have much time."

"I know, honey. Two weeks, if I'm not mistaken. So you're going to have to trust mummy."

****

The letter that landed on the doormat the next morning was the falling leaf that told of the coming storm. The simplicity of its wording brought all the chill of winter with it and would prove how right her forecast had been.

Back in fourteen days

She had wondered whether she should call Ben Logan when the nightmare came and then wondered why she was wondering. He didn't belong to the psychic police; wasn't going to leap into her subconscious and solve everything; nor was that what she had needed as she lay holding her daughter at the nadir of the low-ebb hours and listening to the house creaking around her. The sleep deprivation was enough of a problem in itself, but it was something she could handle and was used to. The nightmare, however, had been a challenge too far.

But the letter should have been proof enough to everyone that Jack Geddis was an immediate danger. Of course he needed an accomplice to push the letter through, but where there was a will there was a way.

Yes, all in all, the scene was tailor-made for a hero and she knew just the man. It would help that his desire for her was written into his every tic, gesture and impulse. And as for her own, dangerously growing attraction to him; there was no disguising or avoiding that, but if he was taking unfair advantage of his DCI role to fan those flames then why shouldn't she use it – use him…"? She would close her mind to accusations of immorality for the moment.

She would need to be careful; after all, as far as anyone knew, Richard was still only missing…

Only missing – an interesting choice of words.

…and she didn't need a scandal in deepest, judgemental Cornwall. Her time in France had almost been enough to see her labelled as some sort of female libertine, even by some members of her family, and caused waves bigger than anything found in the still waters off Mevagissey, so what chance her reputation surviving this latest episode? Also, there remained the issue of Cissie and her unspoken, almost telepathic mistrust of Logan's presence in the house, but now, given the situation it was inarguably preferable for the child to be elsewhere. Claire would call her mother in Truro. That should be far enough away to be safe. At least until the matter of Jack Geddis was resolved.

****

It was as if she had no control over her hips. Christ, they hadn't even removed any clothes yet. In the silence of the lounge Claire's heart raged. She drove her pelvis up against the pressure of his hand.

In the end it had been easier than she'd hoped to push from her mind thoughts of that night in the woods. Perhaps it helped that she wasn't naked.

Here it came. One more squeeze of his hand and her body shuddered. She bit his shoulder to stifle her cries. God, how long had that orgasm been building – since…

Richard.

She knew that the sudden stiffening of her body must have transmitted itself through his fingertips, because the pleasuring hand, which had been working its way to the top of her trousers, stopped. For a moment she wondered whether she had uttered her husband's name as her mind had played its obtuse trick.

This was so hard. There was such a deep need for this physical release that part of her urged that hand to continue its journey. At one point in her life, shivering in an abandoned quarry, she would never have thought that the ashes would re-ignite, or that if they did, that they could ever truly warm her again. There had been some moments of cold fire with Richard, but was this moment the proof that the flames would never again give off heat?

Claire turned her face away from Ben and put the back of her hand across her eyes. It was, literally, a heavy-handed attempt to shield them from view. She had seen the looks from Freddy a few days before, with their questions and concern. They told her that her mind was a box of fine china which had been dropped in transit. Everyone could hear the result, but no-one dared to open it and have a proper look.

"Ben, I'm sorry."

He stroked her hair, puffed out his cheeks and then sat up. "It's ok."

It would have been better to see a lie in his face, but there was nothing. Her tears started.

"I didn't mean...to lead you on."

There was a sad smile on his face as he replied: "I do understand, you know, frustrated though I might be. Cissie doesn't like me."

"Nonsense...it's nothing to do..."

"Claire, it's understandable. I'm not her father. He's missing. Nothing's been put to rest. Even if, or when, the case is closed, it may not bring closure for either of you. And now you're faced with the prospect of your attacker walking free. It's no wonder you're tense."

Claire smiled and put a hand on his cheek. She hadn't told him about the latest nightmares, for any number of reasons, but she had shown him the letter. A look of amazed doubt had been his immediate response and then he had been as supportive as she'd known he would be. That was when she had lowered her defences; to an extent. But she wasn't prepared to let him see how many pieces of china were broken. Not yet. Not till she was ready.

She had to admit that was part of the reason Cissie had not yet been sent away to her mother, even though the latter had agreed to take her without hesitation. Her daughter's presence in the house afforded Claire some defence against complete surrender to Logan. Also she had refused twenty-four hour police protection, telling Logan it was to avoid frightening the little girl, though the reality was different. If her would-be lover wanted to interpret it as a gesture of defiance – a last stand for self-reliance – then that was his prerogative. But it was a calculated risk. Geddis was still in jail. He couldn't harm her yet and Claire didn't want Logan getting his feet under the table before it was a necessity. She needed some room for manoeuvre.

13

The countdown had continued, with letters arriving daily containing the same message; only the number of days changed – they were down to eight. They arrived at different times of day. The plain-clothes men – Logan had now insisted there had to be a permanent presence on the road at least – were puzzled. Okay, they were not based in the house or grounds, but with their vantage point covering the front of the property and an electronic trip system installed at the back they couldn't understand how the mystery mailman was slipping through the net.

Logan expressed concern that the random delivery times increased the chances of Cissie finding a letter. She may not have understood the contents, but as a precocious child she would know something was wrong. Claire suspected it was his way of suggesting Cissie should be sent away. *All in good time,* thought Claire; *everything comes to he, or she, who waits.*

Round and round went Claire's mind, returning always to thoughts of a trammelled future in which the man who had ruined her life walked free, while she sat in a cell of his making; her freedom taken by his sudden need for her and by Fate's aleatoric choice of her as the target when his mind short-circuited. There was no way this could have a happy ending. If revenge was a dish best served cold, five years was a dangerous cooling-off period.

However, although the imminent release of Jack Geddis was the substantive danger, it was the other countdown – the one in Cissie's dreams – which was eroding Claire's sanity. She wondered how much dark knowledge the mind of a child could contain before it seeped through, staining the fabric of their lives forever; while each night the shadow crept closer, and the threat of the dreams grew darker. She could feel one more fibre of her nerves fraying every time she woke in a cold sweat to find Cissie's screams echoing still in the room. At times she could have sworn she was the one screaming as that terrible dragging sound rasped at her scalp. Night after night the little girl stood at the window, hands slapping the glass as she shouted warnings about the thing beyond the cliff edge. This in turn would remind Claire that the last thing she remembered before bursting awake was looking up at the little girl in the window from the garden, hearing her muffled cries, while half-expecting a hand to drop over her own shoulder from behind and grasp her breast.

And out of nothing, or desperation – final shoots of the same dying branch – Claire had an idea.

****

The long-anticipated news put that idea on temporary hold. The dreaded moment had arrived, though she'd not imagined it would come by phone.

"Say that again…Where?…I'm sorry, I don't know how to feel about this." She put her palm to her forehead, trying to stay calm, but continued to press the handset hard against her ear. "How did he…how did it happen?" She had to sit now; it was proving tough, even though she had run through this moment so many times in her mind. She slumped into the chair by the phone. "But that's just down the road from here? How come it's taken till now…oh, I see…who was it?"

****

"They didn't leave their name…Claire, did he have any enemies? Well, we can't rule out that it was foul play until they've completed the post mortem…you know, he was a successful businessman; they usually upset someone on the way up, though admittedly not normally with such consequences. I'm sorry to ask. In fact, Claire…I'm sorry – also for breaking protocol in this way; you should be informed in person by two officers, but I'm stuck in London this evening at a bloody seminar and I wanted you to hear it from me first, given our…well, you know. Anyway, they're on their way. I've been notified that standard procedures are under way and the area's been taped off. They've recovered the vehicle from the water and forensics are making a preliminary examination, but at first glance it does look like he lost control and went over the edge, although why he took that lane is beyond me as the road was diverted quite some time ago.

"I guess what makes me suspicious is why we get this anonymous tip-off now, just a few days before Geddis is due out. Claire, I'm sorry about this, but in due course we will need you to come and formally identity the body. And I warn you now, it won't be easy…well, there's no delicate way to put this, but the vehicle fell a long way, and then the body's obviously been in the water a while. We were lucky to find it so close to where…I'm sorry; that's a terrible choice of words. Jesus, Claire, what can I say? I will get back as quickly as I can – but the guys on site told me quite a crowd had gathered already, even in that remote spot, so obviously news travels fast and I wanted to get to you before some local newshound or busybody did. By the way, I'm not going to give up badgering you to allow me to put an officer in the grounds. As I've broken with protocol already, when I finally have my way, that officer will be me."

****

It was like something out of 'A Nightmare on Elm Street'; she was dosing herself up on caffeine, though it would have been a miracle if Claire could actually have slept, given everything. Of course, coffee wasn't an option for Cissie, nor was inflicting the news about Richard's body for the moment, but she could tell the little girl didn't want to go to bed. Still, at last her daughter's eyelids started to droop and it was time to put her desperate plan into action. Anything was worth trying – especially if it might save them both from the consequences of any further revelations. Her hope lay in how susceptible Cissie had proved to be to hypnosis.

They were lying on the bed, holding each other. The night was clear; through the window they could see stars and a waxing moon, creating a magical feel and making it hard to believe that all was not well in the universe. She stroked Cissie's hair.

"Sweetheart, we're going to create our own bedtime story tonight. With a bit of luck, it will help us keep the nightmares and the monsters away."

Though the girl was drowsy and already stepping across the border into sleep, she gave a little smile and a mumble of consent. It sounded like a good idea to her. Claire felt a stab of guilt at that smile. There was never going to be a good time to tell Cissie about her father, but Claire hadn't finished processing her own feelings about it yet, nor come to terms with them. In the modern world, people had forgotten, perhaps had never even known, the true darkness of the land of Nod.

"We're going to the pretty place, my darling; the one which the nasty shadow tries to destroy. Can you see it?"

"Yes, mummy. But I can see…"

"I know sweetheart, but we mustn't let that spoil it. Do you know what we're going to do?"

"No mummy."

"We're going to build a wall; a nice wall of shiny white stones, with turrets and flags along the top, just like the castle in the distance. We're going to build our own castle and inside the walls will be a waterfall, and butterflies, and meadows with horses. And the sun will always shine. Are you going to help me?"

The girl smiled, even though her eyes were closed and her voice dreamy. "Yes, mummy."

"And you'll see; the shadow won't get through or over the wall. It will have to stay outside, huffing and puffing, but it won't get in. You and I will be safe. Can you see the white horses, darling?"

"Yes."

"They're coming towards us."

"But so is the..."

Claire cut in again, as if the darkness was the Candyman and mentioning it would strengthen it. "I know, sweetheart, I know. But look how we're taking a stone and putting it down. A magic stone. Here's another. Can you help mummy lift this stone? It's heavy." The girl frowned, but with effort, not fear. "It's a big stone, isn't it?"

"It is."

"Is it making you tired?"

"Tired – yes." The voice was growing croaky with fatigue.

"But look at how big the wall is already. Let's get some more stones."

The girl managed one more white stone before her breathing became deeper and more rhythmic, but Claire continued to build, her mind focused on picturing that task to the exclusion of all else – almost. All she saw were her hands lifting stones and placing them on top of others, but she couldn't blot out the sounds; the approaching footfall and the accompanying dragging. She knew that every night that wall would have to be built higher. And not simply to keep out whatever was on the other side. Another voice was urging her to clamber to the top and look. She feared that voice more than the one that muttered and hissed its threats in the land of Nowhere.

Strange how, despite the lingering doubts, mother and daughter both fell into a sound sleep that night.

They woke to a different world.

14

For a start, the letters stopped.

Ben Logan continued his call-by at some point each day, however, so some things hadn't changed. It wasn't his fault, on reflection, that his presence was more disturbing than reassuring; it was just hard to be sociable with someone when they'd had their hand between your legs, an event followed by your husband's body rising from its watery grave.

It had shocked her blood to ice at the morgue.

Just on a physical level, she was tempted to surrender more of herself – she could have used the release it might have provided – but the time wasn't right, for all manner of reasons. Despite everything, she knew very little about him, apart from the mild compulsions he sought to mask and the way his eyes seemed always to slide away from her face. When they did talk, the main topics of discussion didn't make for relaxed chatter either.

Three days before Geddis was due out, the cracks were starting to show.

"The forensic team has…" Logan hesitated, trying to find an appropriate turn of phrase, "…a lot of work to do on the damaged body, so there won't be a funeral in a hurry."

"In its own way that's a relief." Claire squeezed her fingers against her eyes. "I'm not sure I could cope with that on top of everything else at the moment."

Logan sipped the coffee. "At least the countdown letters have stopped. The increased police presence must have put off the perpetrator."

"Doesn't that raise a host of other questions, since we're talking plain-clothes officers in unmarked cars?" It surprised her to see he had not thought that one through; the signet ring spun on his finger; Claire had noticed how, when things – control, in particular – ran away from Logan, he seemed to use the ring to reel them back in. "Smacks of inside information, doesn't it, that the mystery postman hasn't tried again?"

He shifted in his seat; uncomfortable. "I suppose we can't rule that out, although let's not forget I've been nearby too. But I'm sure no-one in the force has any dealings with Geddis."

"Who said anything about Geddis?" She couldn't keep the sarcasm from her voice. "Some might say if you want a well-organised, well-informed raving sicko, look no further than the people who understand that mind-set best. Don't they say, set a thief to catch a thief?"

"My team are entirely trustworthy," snapped Logan, seeming not to like the way the conversation was heading.

"Maybe Geddis has a girlfriend; someone of the Myra Hindley school – faithful…"

"Obedient." The word was out before Logan knew it.

Claire caught herself wondering whether Logan preferred his women subservient – a bit less feisty than her perhaps – but before she knew it she was hit by a flash image of herself, bound, helpless and on her knees in the woods. Her chest constricted. The war of the sexes had become a dangerous game of chess and she was no longer sure she knew or understood the rules. Jack Geddis had not bothered explaining them when he had moved the first piece, but the only certainty was there could be no winners.

Logan was looking at her, irritated, but whether by her criticism or his own loss of control, she couldn't tell. He pushed ahead anyway. "Someone who's stayed faithful and out of jail, laying low till he sent her a signal a few days before his release to..." He ground to a halt, too late to prevent the conversation's momentum leading it to its inevitable conclusion.

Claire said the words he'd tried to avoid: "...to scare the living daylights out of the woman who got her man sent to jail."

Ben raised a placatory hand. "However, as there was no mention of a girlfriend during the investigation or trial, we might be allowing our imagination to run away with us."

Claire looked long and hard at him. "Ever been tied up and made to kneel naked on the cold earth in the middle of nowhere, DCI Logan, with a stinking sack tied over your head, waiting for rape, death or both, while a madman watches you in silence? Don't talk to me about imagination; you haven't the faintest idea what it is."

As conversation stoppers went it was up there with the double-barrel shotgun. She saw the hurt in his face, but for now her well of sympathy was dry. Claire could not bring herself to apologise, so she did the next best thing, which was to carry on talking as if nothing had happened.

"Look, a third party might not exist, but, directly or indirectly, this is being driven by Jack Geddis. It ties in absolutely with his release date. He's coming out and something or someone has got it in for me as a result."

He nodded, reflecting. "Still, it's pretty sparsely populated around here; not the sort of place you head for unless you live here or have an agenda. My men should have spotted and observed anyone using this road. But you won't let me station anyone in the grounds and so that leaves ways in, and if you're obsessed enough you'll find one of those ways. They say love is blind, but there's also blind obsession."

He looked at her and, for once, she couldn't read his eyes.

Or chose not to.

****

In the midst of the storm that was her life right then, Claire had at least found some solidity; her self-styled dream therapy seemed to be working. Both she and Cissie were managing some sleep. The footsteps and ominous dragging sound hadn't gone away – in fact they were getting closer – but the wall was rising, and safe behind it they got through to dawn.

****

She had willed it to be so. Her absolute terror of it happening had created it. The police had taken the letters but couldn't find any forensic evidence. Perhaps, they had been manifestations of her subconscious, made real by her own hand. Freddy just about stopped short of telling her that she was suffering a form of schizophrenia and had arranged for the letters to be sent.

On the surface, this was just another therapeutic chat with her friend. That she'd continued with these informal sessions was as much down to friendship as any acceptance that she needed her anchor in the turbulent waters of her life, but today Freddy was sensing a different agenda. He couldn't nail it. Even as she told him about her apparent success in staving off the nightmares, she seemed guarded – closed and disingenuous, he thought – so he had decided to stir things up; shake off some soil and see whether he couldn't expose the root.

She stared at him in dismay as he made his comments.

"Don't be so ridiculous, Freddy!"

He didn't flinch in the slightest as she turned on him, having reinforced his own defences; her latent anger would neither undermine nor wrong-foot him this time. "It's a form of auto-suggestion; your whole moral justification for being depends, at this time, on the reality of what's happening to you. You need it to be real, because the alternative is, well, that you're imagining it – and we don't want to start down that path."

She was perched on the very edge of the chair, seething. "I don't see that that path exists."

Freddy raised just one finger for emphasis. "Precisely; you don't see it. Or your frontal cortex doesn't want you to. You refuse to believe that you concocted the whole thing when your hormones were all messed up and you were two months pregnant by a man you believed no longer loved you."

"How dare…!"

"And you drove yourself to that quarry, set all the wheels in motion, or at least set fire to them, then staggered home, devoid of semen or any other stains, which you had conveniently washed away. But when Richard still didn't love you enough, his disappearance enabled you to bring back into your life Detective Chief Inspector Ben Logan, a man you knew from your previous dealings was hooked on you and who had cooked up a case and sacrificed five years of an innocent man's life just to give you credence. Now the two of you had a bona fide reason to spend time together, while you salved your conscience by citing your husband's disappearance and concern for your child's state of mind as a reason not to be intimate with him. Still you can have him around; these letters provide a perfect, valid excuse."

She sat with her mouth open; stunned.

It had taken Freddy all his will-power to play devil's advocate and deliver that without looking away. Now he held out his hands, palms upwards and shrugged. "I'm just looking at the scenario from all sides; trying to imagine I'm not your friend."

"Well you won't have to imagine too hard." That hurt him, despite everything, and it seemed she noticed, drawing strength from his discomfort. "Stop playing with me, Freddy, I'm not a laboratory rat."

"I'm not playing with you, Claire. Surely only friends play." Now she stiffened, and Freddy felt ashamed as the word *touché* crossed his mind.

As a man who preferred to evict chaos and emotion from living rent-free in his brain, he tried to get back on track and stay focused. "But I am indulging in a bit of reverse psychology."

Her eyes narrowed. "Explain."

He remained motionless, which had always been his way of ensuring patients were not distracted from his words. "I see an anger in you when you visit me now – a cold fire – that didn't exist even in the immediate aftermath of the attack. Oh, I knew you could slam doors, like anyone else, particularly in the faces of people you care about. It's a way of building an immediate physical barrier to save them from getting hurt. But this is different. You can't slam a door in your own face. I can't yet fathom the defensive guilt, but guilt there is. So please believe me, I'm trying to help." She snorted and he ignored her. "To help," he re-emphasised, "by putting to you even the most outlandish scenarios, so you can see them and choose to discard them. Then maybe we can get to the nub of this."

She stayed bolt upright on the chair, but something had changed. At first Freddy didn't recognise the nature of it, but it was there, as tangible and yet indefinable as the moment the tide turns. Claire was different; he couldn't read her that well any more. And that was when it struck him; for maybe the first time in his professional capacity Freddy felt he had no control. He had exposed the roots all right – and it seemed they might be rotten. It would have been better if he'd never caused the old memories to stir via his hypnosis of Cissie.

Jack Geddis, what have we done to her?

They said nothing for a while. He stared at her; she stared back. Then Claire rose, crossed to where he was seated and, with a sudden smile, gestured for him to stand.

"I guess I should thank you." With that, she slapped him hard across the face. He staggered with the force of it. "At least now I'm in touch with my cold anger."

She turned on her heel and left the room. Another door slammed.

Freddie took his hand from his face and looked at it, half-expecting to see blood perhaps; shocked to the absolute core. That their friendship might be at an end was the last thing he'd planned. Now he was going to have to find another way.

15

It was the Cornwall about which they don't tell tourists in the brochures; all the home fires that might be burning hidden for now behind the rise and fall of the land, beyond the car windows, against which the rain was being hurled in a right hook rather than a series of jabs. Despite the half mile between them and the coast, and even with the car windows closed, they could hear the spite of huge rollers thumping their frustration against the cliffs in the eternal heavyweight contest. Further down the coast, by Newquay and St. Ives, there would still be a few nutters trying to surf those waves whatever the weather and time of day or night, even minus any moonlight, but not here; not if they didn't want to end up splatted like mosquitoes against rocks and cliffs.

Only a madman would be out in this – and of course the men who were trying to catch him. Then again, a madman was what they were up against; a calculating one, judging by events; the worst kind.

The appearance of headlights round the corner snapped Detective Inspector Heath and Detective Constable Donaldson out of the drudgery that was their watch duty that night. Excitement was at a premium at the best of times on the Cornish peninsular, never mind in the winter season when everything was shut down, but on this lonely stretch of road, unlit, with barely any traffic and the leaden skies of earlier that day delivering on their promise of rain, the words *straw* and *short* sprang to mind. Hence the approach of the lights was a moment of rare drama, but the friendly double-flash of the beams told a different story.

Still, at least the boredom would now be broken by getting something to eat.

The squad car pulled alongside, windows were wound down, at which point the noise of those demonic waves filled the air with threats while rain attempted its invasion of the interior.

"There you go." PC Trebayne almost threw the two bags in before winding his window back up till only a sliver of glass-free space remained. "Nothing happening?" he shouted through the gap.

The gusts were blowing from the passenger side of Heath's car and he was in the driver's seat, so he kept his window a little lower. "This goes beyond nothing. Thanks mate. Enjoy your snooze at the station."

The squad car headed off while Donaldson busied himself trying to balance the various greasy suppers on whatever surfaces he could find. Heath left his window cracked open; no matter what your food tastes, few people liked getting into a car that smelt of takeaway. He counted himself in that category; these burgers were not his choice. As he stared at the rivulets of rain which had turned the windscreen opaque and then took in the contents of the takeaway packs, which as usual bore little resemblance to the pictures on the website, he had further reason to curse Logan. Not that the DCI had assigned him to this job; his own suspicions and a lingering sense of disquiet had laid that particular curse.

It seemed his mood hadn't escaped his colleague. "Given what you just said and the shitty weather, I'm surprised you decided to take this shift, sir."

Heath gathered himself together. "Never harms to treat yourself to a reminder of real policework; keep yourself grounded and sharpen the wits. Besides, DC Watkins and his missus are trying for a family. Thought he might appreciate an evening in to try a bit… harder, if you get my drift!" He hoped the leering tone of the last words would put his old mucker Donaldson off the track and onside.

It seemed to have worked. "Talking of which, what d'you reckon?" Donaldson grinned, gesturing with his eyebrows past Heath towards the iron gates while he handed over several unmanageable sachets of ketchup to the senior officer.

"I reckon we've no chance of seeing anything tonight…or any other night. Whoever this guy is, he's delivered several letters already. Wouldn't be surprised if he's shinning up the cliffs – he's obviously pretty determined."

Donaldson shovelled a chunk of burger into his mouth and then asked the muffled question: "Really, I meant do you reckon he's fucking her?"

The word *fucking* came out literally gluten- and grease-laden. Heath brushed discretely at his suit jacket in distaste, raised his eyebrows: "You mean Logan? I doubt he knows how."

"Go ooon!" The second word was prolonged with suggestiveness. "He caught her attacker, banged him up, her husband's conveniently driven himself off a cliff and now he's calling in to see her most days, taking…" he parenthesised with air commas "… *personal responsibility* for her safety. Of course he is. Don't blame him. On a scale of nought to one I'd give her one!" Donaldson's hearty laughter at his own pun morphed into a voluminous burp.

The burger, which had been halfway to Heath's mouth paused there as the DI looked at his colleague and shook his head at his table manners. "Well, as long as she didn't mind not getting so much as a 'good morning' at breakfast and makes sure every surface in her house is clean enough for surgical procedures, how could any woman resist the charms of our high-flying DCI?" He gently replaced the burger, intact, in its carton and peered in the direction of the house, invisible behind the spattering rain. "I don't doubt he wants to, but setting everything else aside, does she, especially after everything she's been through?"

The last part of the sentence carried particular emphasis and Donaldson looked suitably chastened.

Heath continued: "Besides, I don't know with him. I've never warmed to him."

"No-one down at the station would blame you for that, I tell you. Did you know he walked right past Watkins in the street last weekend and totally blanked him …as if the poor lad wasn't feeling bad enough already with that bloody awful new haircut he'd just got! I had you nailed on for the DCI job. What the hell they bring him down from Hampshire for?"

Heath had steeled himself anew to take a bite of his burger, but once again he paused and returned it to the foam container. "Yes, what I still don't get – I don't mean about me being passed over – just him…I mean, why him? Okay, he's got a decent track record, but why did old Daniel Rawlings suddenly transfer him across? I know Rawlings well enough to know he's a politician. That transfer would have been to his benefit, but whether in a positive way, or because he was throwing out some rubbish, perhaps some toxic waste, I don't know."

Heath looked over his shoulder and then closed his window. Donaldson gave him a quizzical look. "I don't know what you're about to tell me, but I assure you there's no fucker here to overhear you."

Heath shrugged and gave a slight grin. "True enough – but look; I did a bit of asking around. No-one knows much about Logan. He really keeps himself to himself; doesn't socialise, as you know. No-one's ever been to his place. I couldn't get anything about his days before he joined the police. But his last case in Hampshire…well, there's something odd about it. It looked like the investigation was over, but it refused to die."

"Meaning what?"

"Wish I knew. I've no other details right now. It's as if the file's been airbrushed." He stared into the rain. "Rawlings again?"

"Well, whatever else, he really found the key to nail that bastard Geddis in this case didn't he?"

Heath picked a single fry out of the container and looked at it thoughtfully. "Even that – I don't know; there's something about it." He popped the fry into his mouth and chewed it with a lack of enthusiasm. "Almost too convenient, if you ask me, like someone just wanted the file closed and had Geddis to do it with." He looked across at Donaldson.

"But it was pretty sharp of him to ask for those extra tests."

Heath pulled a sceptical face; tilted his head from side to side. "Yeaaah, I suppose. Maybe forensics should have run those tests at the time, but you could say the same about a thousand other million-to-one shot tests they didn't run from that scene, so how did Logan go straight to it? Seems he studied Forensic Science himself at University, though I found no…" For once, Donaldson's hoovering up of the first of his two nightly milk-shakes was a blessing in disguise, as the last words were drowned out and it allowed Heath to change tack. "…I'm told the records of Logan's qualification that we should have on file got misplaced on their way over from Hampshire, but Rawlings backed him, so I guess I've got to allow for it – but…" He dropped his hands into his lap and gave a big sigh, "…I dunno. I don't like it and I've got to say I don't like him. Problem is, people will think it's just sour grapes…" he stared forward again, "…but you know me of old, Pete, so if you ever hear anything…"

That seemed to set the tone for the night. They finished the takeaway in a relative silence, broken only by Donaldson's digestive system as they peered in hopeless anticipation into the darkness.

****

Logan parked up and started to meander across the road in the dappled morning light, which would have made a mockery of any tales of the storm from the previous night, if it weren't for the remnants of standing water at the roadside. He headed towards the house, in front of which sat the unmarked surveillance car. He didn't bother to look right or left before crossing the road; it was so quiet here, a vehicle would have to be coasting along in neutral not to be heard.

His phone rang.

Her voice never failed to make the base of his spine tingle. Would she always have that power? He needed that to change. "Hi Claire…what's wrong? What! Are you sure? Well yes, I don't doubt you're holding a piece of paper, but…look, I'm just out on the road. I'll be with you in a minute."

He walked at a much quicker pace now to the other car. One of the officers had his window wound down. "Morning…sir."

The voice shocked him, though he hid it well enough. That hint of disrespect in the officer's use of 'sir' could only emanate from one man. "Morning…Inspector Heath." Two could play at that game; though he shouldn't have, he enjoyed administering the little reminder of rank. More importantly though, what the hell was Heath doing slumming it on a stake-out? Logan assumed DC Donaldson would be the other officer; the two men were long time compadres and he had never managed to break into the clique. "Quiet night?"

"Like a churchyard." Heath's features evinced concern despite his confident answer; perhaps he had picked up from the tone of Logan's response to the phone call that something might have gone tits-up.

"Mmm, well, just like a churchyard, I've a feeling we might have a ghost."

"How d'you mean?"

Logan did not give an immediate answer, but glanced into the car. Near the handbrake and in the passenger foot-well by the feet of Detective Constable Donaldson lay various polystyrene and paper containers with the tell-tale logo. "You guys were here the whole time, yes? Watching closely?"

Heath had noted the direction of Logan's gaze. "Positive, sir. We placed this order by radio to the station and they brought it out."

Logan snorted. "Good use of tax-payer's money." They might have thought he was being a prick, that he'd surely done the same thing himself on many a stake-out, even in the la-di-da environs of Winchester, but, in this instance, he felt the need to establish a little authoritative distance; ensure his men didn't lose their grip on the precious cargo through not taking him seriously. Logan had always done his best, within the restrictions of his prosopagnosia to maintain the illusion of being a team-player, but that could be mistaken for weakness once you'd moved up the promotional ladder. One needed to maintain respect.

The thought did occur to him that he might be over-compensating for other things that seemed beyond his power to moderate. He tried to dismiss the notion. Imposing order was second nature to him in the world beyond the gaze of his peers.

"It gets a bit cold in the early hours, sir. Not sure what it's like in rural Hampshire, but out here on the north coast…"

"I'm from these parts, Heath." This was the last thing Logan needed – getting drawn into a petty squabble with another officer. Nor did his facial blindness prevent him from sensing Donaldson's approval for his night-shift partner.

Heath hadn't finished though. "We've always trusted our lads to be able to keep focus on the job, even if they're having a quick bite to keep warm. And we're diligent about not wasting taxpayers' money. Not sure if you know, sir, but PC Trebayne lives right by the takeaway and comes over this way when he heads to the station to start his shift, so he's not having to go out of his way to bring us a bite. Besides…" Logan caught Heath's glance towards Donaldson, "…we thought you might also be …on the job, sir. Checking everything was right inside."

Logan chose not to swallow the obvious bait. He had ammunition of his own and brandished the phone. "Well I wasn't, Heath. If I had been, she wouldn't have received another letter."

Heath's brows furrowed. "What, she phoned you just now?"

"Yes, just now. You saw me answer…"

"I only meant that she seemed fine when she popped out this morning, sir."

"Popped out?" Logan looked at the phone as if it had become hot.

"Oh, she's back now. Wasn't out for too long. And whoever it is didn't trip any of the detectors we've got round the sides and back and can't have got past us here on the road, I swear to you. The station records will show we called in every thirty minutes – there's been no falling asleep on the job here, sir."

"Hmmm." He realised he was looking up towards the house and not really listening to them.

"That's a fair-sized perimeter she's got there, and if the detectors aren't enough to cover the back and we can't put men inside the grounds you're going to need a helicopter patrol to be sure no-one gets near the place, sir."

Were they laughing at him? Perhaps they were right to. His first question should have been whether there'd been any activity of any sort, including this morning. His thoughts of Claire were affecting his skills as a policeman.

"So what, you think some member of the SAS parachuted in, left the letter then used a jetpack to get over the infra-red detector grids at the back before abseiling down the cliffs?"

Perhaps Donaldson sensed the growing tension, because he decided to enter the conversation. "It's got to be something outside the normal, sir. Those detectors will go off if anything moves within ten feet of the ground anywhere round the sides or back, and if someone came past our car to get to the front we'd have seen them – especially this morning even if they were dressed in camouflage." Logan had the grace to smile, partly because they didn't know how close they were to the truth. "Anyway, sir, never mind how; *why* would Geddis be doing this? He's got to have enough sense to stay away from her."

Heath chipped in. "Mind you, he likes to scare her. That's what he did before. Maybe the thought of frightening her is helping him to whack off in his cell."

With a curt nod to the two detectives, but no further comment, Logan headed for the gates. Heath was right; there was no logic to Geddis' actions so close to his release and Logan needed Claire to drop her guard – let him in – if he was to find out what was going on.

****

She almost threw herself into his arms.

"God, Ben, I'm so scared."

Taken aback, he held her; resisted the overwhelming urge to stroke her hair. The smell of her! It took all his self-control.

"Why's he doing this, Ben?"

Why are you doing this? he wanted to ask. Was it as simple as fear driving her into another protector's embrace? He sensed nothing about her was uncomplicated. In so many ways she was like every mirror he had ever looked into, presenting a reflection he knew but couldn't recognise. Hard though it would be, he would have to remind himself: along with his need for her there was a need to be careful.

"*How's* he doing it?" She modified her own question. "I thought you guys were supposed to protect me." She looked up at him; her face moist. "I…I'm not sure I can take much more of this. The attack; Richard's disappearance; Richard's…the discovery of the body; this victimisation. Society's supposed to protect people like me. He may have been in a cell for going on five years, but I don't know whether I'll ever be free." She put both hands to his face. "And then on top of it all, there's you." Perhaps realising her words were both revelatory and ambiguous, she moved her hands down to his chest. He knew his thundering heart would be sending its message through her fingers. "I'm sorry – I didn't want that last part to sound negative. Despite everything that's happened to me these last years and every atom of any common sense telling me to be careful, I can't help that I've started to care about you, but I'm scared; of what people might think of me if they believe I'm seeing you – and Richard not yet even buried. I'm not even sure what I think of myself. Am I some sort of slut? Have I brought this on myself? Did I provoke Jack Geddis somehow, that he did this to me and continues to bear me this hatred?"

Logan was now more than taken aback; he was nervous. It seemed that Geddis' vengeance was an ill wind blowing her into his arms. She had not thrown herself at him in this way before. Yes, they'd had an encounter that ended up being intimate, but it had felt like two people attracted to each other letting down their guard in a moment of abandonment. He had to be careful, particularly from a professional point of view. It was one thing to long for, perhaps lust after something or someone you were pretty confident could never be yours, but this…?

This changed everything and not necessarily for the good.

Yet he wanted her so very much.

He had a sudden image of his sister and all the damage she had caused, with and without intent. The word *slut* from Claire's lips had kicked the hornet's nest again.

He took Claire by the shoulders. "This is typical; and you must stop it now. So many victims of sexual assault go through this part of the process where they start to blame themselves."

And then, no more words. Her mouth was on his; hungry again, needy, and just as abrupt in its removal. As an encapsulation of everything it was perfect.

"Look at me," she said, "what am I doing?" Logan glanced past her towards the stairs. She caught the direction of his gaze. "I took her away this morning to my mum's. She needs to be far from here."

"What, you're just going to stay here on your own? You should stay there with her." He hoped his hollow words echoed with concern.

"No, Ben; with typical perversity I've decided that I need to be here. If I'm going to come through this I need to not be driven away from my home. Otherwise he wins."

With all the strength he had ever channelled into keeping his tics and obsessions caged, Logan fought to ensure his next words sounded tight and professional. "Well, you know what; I warned you I'm not going to let you rattle around in here and certainly not on your own for the next two nights. I'm going to be here. I'll stick my car right outside your door in addition to the usual two officers by the gate and the detectors around the perimeter. As I mentioned before, it's bucking procedures, but with this count-down nearing its conclusion, something outside the box is needed. If I'm breaking the rules, then I'll clock off and be here as a friend, invited by you. And that's not all I'm going to do." He put his hands on her shoulders and looked right into her eyes. "I'm going to take care of this for you." She placed her hand on his chest. He knew she would be reading the telemetry of his particular needs through her fingertips. It was time to act at last. "Geddis is not going to bother you again."

As he walked away from the house, Logan's thoughts from a few minutes before found an echo. His dealings with Claire meant he was walking a dangerous road. Now, something was indeed coasting in neutral behind him along that shadowy track; picking up speed as it careered downhill, out of control. He was too scared to look around.

****

If Logan had actually looked around as he left the house, he would not have seen any conflict in Claire's features. However, once she had closed the door she leaned back against it and breathed out, the stream of air shaking through lips which had fought so hard to simulate a loving smile. A couple of deep breaths and she had recovered enough to say to herself: "There, that wasn't so hard, was it?" Except that it had been. The seductress had never been a role she'd needed or wanted to play. Surrendering her body as part of a plan had not been key to her vision of life as a young girl. Some women might have been only too thrilled by the thought of using sex as a tool to hoodwink a man, but while Claire could not deny the physical nature of the act was pleasurable in a limited way, her fears, released from their box in the woods on that night, still danced around her. She was using Logan to keep a beast at bay, but in doing so, was she allowing another monster into her life? The next day or so would tell.

She felt a smile forming, but it was full of irony and weariness. She had always wanted to get to know a man before she would sleep with him; now she was going to sleep with one in order to get to know him.

16

Dartmoor Prison; a black hole. It didn't look to have changed much since the days when pirates and other criminals were subjected to public hangings.

When he had first moved back to Cornwall, Logan had chosen not to skirt around Dartmoor on the journey, but cross part of it using the B-roads. Its bleak beauty appealed to him. In fact, he believed it was a place best enjoyed in solitude. Part of that stemmed, as for so many people, from a love of *The Hound of the Baskervilles*. Also, it resonated with Logan that Sherlock Holmes was a solitary character whose forensic skills, allied with an ability to inhabit the mind of the criminal, enabled him to flow through the veins of the underworld. But it was so much more than that. Dartmoor was timeless, beautiful, ancient and unforgiving. It lived as it wished and meted out punishment to the unwary. He liked that – a world of unequivocal, primitive justice. He had felt like he was heading back to where he belonged as he passed through.

The jail was a carbuncle on the austere beauty of the moor's face, yet fed the darkness of its reputation. Its existence still held appeal from a Conan Doyle perspective, given its mention in *The Hound of the Baskervilles*, but it was further proof that man was incapable of blending beauty with punishment. As he drove towards it now,

Logan noted both how the granite walls dominated the landscape of that area and how stone could elicit such differing emotions; how fashioned by nature in this wilderness it would cause the ancient streams to babble, or stand proud and imposing in the abstract majesty of Dartmoor's tors; how hewn and ordered by man, it spoke of conquest and captivity.

That last word caused him to shudder. He imagined how different it would feel to approach this place in the back of a prison van facing years, possibly the rest of one's life here. Then the landscape he had thought of as having bleak nobility just moments before would condense to simply bleak.

Now, from the more civilised side of the reinforced glass in the visiting area Logan looked around at the ubiquitous, institutional green paint while he waited for Geddis to be brought through and felt a cold sweat forming on his forehead as he reflected; if the lid were ever lifted off his past to reveal all its secrets he could find himself on the wrong side of that glass.

He ought to have felt worse for the man he had come to see, but he didn't; he really didn't. Not with what he knew. Both inside and outside the prison walls, things could have been a lot worse for that fucking pervert. Dartmoor Prison might have been grim, but there were worse places and he'd managed to swing this for Geddis, whose crime of indecent assault might have seen him in a Category A prison instead of this Category C. Logan had argued that given his plea, Geddis was prepared to accept his sentence and unlikely to try to escape. However, there was a surreal element to all of this; each wanted the other's silence and acceptance of how things had turned out. It was almost an ugly truce.

Twenty-three years before

He had always been something of a ghost in the town, but then he had needed to be, given his urges and predilections. It wasn't exactly the sort of thing you shared with your friends and ever since things with that slut – what was her name…Anna? – had got out of hand, he had kept a low profile. To this day he couldn't believe that he hadn't been called in for that police line-up, especially as that weird brother of hers had seen him hurrying away from the scene. After that, he had been as quiet as a mouse; taken a sabbatical of sorts, you might say. And after all, he always had the pictures. They were his treasures. It was why he did what he did. That might have been hard for others to understand, though who a lone wolf like him would be trying to explain it to, he couldn't imagine.

The pictures gave him power; were evidence of that power. A winning smile, a decent camera, a fake photographer's ID and suddenly every girl along the north Cornish coast was a wannabe glamour model cum slut.

Cum slut. He grinned at the unintentional wordplay, but for whatever reason, whatever madness was his – and yes, he acknowledged there was a sickness – watching was his thing, whether through the lens of his camera or alone in the privacy of his home – or at least it had been, till she had tempted him.

When the whores-in-the-making eventually challenged him, demanding to know which magazines had bought the pictures and wanting their cut, finally realising they'd been made fools of in any way that counted, again the photos were his power. There was nothing like the threat of revelation, of a picture through the letter-box at home or at work, or if necessary just a threat, to earn their silence; a lesson they could take forward into life – though once a whore, always a whore, he guessed.

Perhaps he couldn't really blame them. Amidst the endless pounding of the sea, the Atlantic winds, the screeching seagulls, the mists and mindless tourists, the garden-fence gossip, what else did they have to bring some excitement into their small-town lives?

Anna Hammett, on the other hand, had been a mistake in more ways than one; a bit too close to home. Not like his other – what was the right word? – experiments. Typically, he had gone further afield; not shat on his own doorstep. But he had just seen her one day, as if Muldoon town had suddenly sprouted an exotic flower.

He'd slowed the car, watching her walking away from school. He knew he had to have her in his collection and as he drove slowly by her, that little look she gave into the car told him everything he needed to know. Hand on heart, he couldn't tell, didn't know whether she was under age; any man would have been hard-pushed to guess. On reflection, it wouldn't have mattered and after all, he wasn't planning to try to have sex with her. Not planning.

He found out where she lived; tailed her one evening to a bar. Captured in some of his favourite images, the rest was history – ancient history now. She'd been dangerous. He had heard that sometimes, when she went to powder her nose, it meant something other than cosmetics, given she occasionally kept company with a known small-time drug dealer. He hadn't needed to embellish his cover story of glamour photography to get her to pose. She was what sometimes happened when small town thought big.

Against his better judgement, they'd also had a thing for a while – but then she'd changed her mind; wanted the pictures. The argument and what followed – well, he'd thought the game was up, particularly when she threatened to blow his world apart. That and the thought of years behind bars had driven him to the edge, both of them in fact, but rather too literally in her case.

After that, he had gone dark and silent; just his pictures for company. Technology was advancing and in time he bought one of the best laptops. Combined with a digital camera, his secret became much easier to hide. He was able to destroy the old hard copies – an appropriate innuendo thrown up by the new technology – of his 'hot' picture collection.

At last, about four years on, he thought the coast must be clear.

Which was when he started to get the feeling he was being watched. Sometimes, it was just a sense of something. He'd look over his shoulder, not sure whether he'd imagined someone disappearing down an alleyway or into a shop. Now, at the door of his flat, he would always take a bit of time with his keys and use that cover to glance up and down the road, just in case he'd been followed. He might have believed it was his conscience, except clearly a man with his cravings possessed no such thing.

So at last he had settled for it being his imagination.

As he opened his front door that evening, he learnt one thing; never trust your imagination.

****

He had always wanted to blend in, rather than be stared at as Anna's weird brother. How ironic then that at first he had found it uncomfortable when people's eyes slid past him as they sought to avoid him. Eventually though, it suited him fine, once he had learned to deal with the loneliness. There was no better place than the shadows from which to catch a ghost – and he was convinced this was what his prey was trying to be. Of course, he couldn't rely on recognising the man, given his difficulties with face blindness, as he had come to call it after researching his symptoms. He wouldn't have been able to pick him out by his features if they had shared a table in a café, unless there was a striking mole or scar. In fact, his chances would have been better in the anonymity of a confessional box; vocal inflections were one source of differentiation.

Years had passed, so too childhood. Various flames had turned to embers, including such friendships as he'd once had. Still, the need for revenge, for justice glowed somewhere. He may not have pursued it, but he knew the breeze of chance might always set it ablaze again.

As far as the opposite sex was concerned, he had the same hormonal desires as any teenage boy, but no faith. First dates were surprisingly plentiful – girls seemed less shy of talking to him than boys did, many told him he was *a looker* and he was happy to take them at their word, but things rarely got to the relationship stage. There was little chance when demons tagged along, or you walked past your date because she'd changed her hair, whether colour or style, or was wearing something different from the first time you spoke. He discovered he didn't quite have the correct chat when it came to telling girls what to wear for the next liaison! Above all, having witnessed the destructiveness of desire, he found himself repelled by the idea of losing control.

All of which faded into insignificance one day when he caught sight of a particular rust-coloured shirt, the button on the left cuff a poor match for the one on the right.

He had managed to find himself a weekend job waiting tables at a café. The tables had numbers, which were given at the counter when the order was placed and that helped him immensely, not needing to recognise his customers. That particular morning, the man in the distinctive shirt at table 12 was watching a group of female tourists walk by, dressed for the heat of that summer's day. There was something about the way he looked. Later, when he moved on, his rather scuttling walk was as damning as a fingerprint. By that stage, a scar on the back of his neck had been mentally filed away as an added identifier.

The embers flared. He stayed out of their light, managing to avoid serving Scar-Neck in case the latter recognised the waiter as being a potential problem.

During the weeks that followed, whenever he saw that peculiar walk, the shirt, the scar, a distinctive mole that a new haircut had revealed on the back of the ear, he stalked that man, who was a semi-regular at the café, observing his behaviour and routines, but never once questioning his own lack of a plan. The activity itself became a kind of obsession, but also a way of putting off the inevitable. He had once hurled a watch into the sea, scared and confused. Now time had resurfaced, mocking him, because it, history and his own life would stand still unless he found the proof he needed and took the action it demanded.

Now, as he stood in the shadows of a late October evening, watching his target perform his usual scan of the surrounding area from his front door – the actions of a guilty man if ever there were – he knew he needed to get inside that apartment.

It was a relief to have a new focus for a few days. He had taken note and pictures of the type of lock on the apartment door. Part of the money he made waiting tables was spent on buying the same type of lock and then he embarked on a task suited to his ways; learning how to dismantle it, reassemble it so he could understand what made it work. As a metaphor for his life and his interactions with people, this was perfect.

Above all, he needed to open that door – it was possible the rest of his life lay behind it.

****

There is something about the moment you enter your seemingly inviolate home and then realise someone else has been there. Even before the harsh truths crystallize, there is a sense of wrong, the more so if you have something to hide. Perhaps there is a scent, faint, almost undetectable, but alien nonetheless; or an object seems out of place, even though you've always paid little or no attention to it.

Then, at last, a flag of invasion flutters.

He saw the piece of paper on his desk. Lying across it like a threatening paperweight was a letter-opener in the form of a mini-rapier; it was not his own. He shot panic glances around the living space. Everything looked intact, but then he knew it could, even if the most precious, the most dangerous piece had been taken. Striding across to the bookcase, he tore several volumes off the second shelf and his worst fears were realised. The laptop and disks were gone.

Too breathless even to utter the *shits* and *fucks* that entered his head, he realised it might be an idea to look at the note. Just eight words: *Across the street — wear the rust-coloured shirt.*

What the fuck?

He made his shaky way over to the window and saw a figure standing on the opposite pavement. In the autumn gloaming there was a vague familiarity to the face, but no more than that.

The guy waved, just once, the gesture a parody of what it should have meant.

"Rust-coloured shirt...rust-coloured shirt?" he muttered. Then he was hit by a horrendous ecstasy of knowledge and awareness. His legs felt hollow, his stomach empty. That was the shirt...

He stared again at the waiting figure. It might be...it might be him, though he was so much taller now, and better built.

Much as he wanted to go out there and just drive his fist through that face, he was too damned scared and knew that he had better comply. If those disks got into the wrong hands...

When he had pulled on the shirt he left the apartment and crossed the road. He could see already his tormentor didn't have the laptop him. Fuck!!

They stood facing each other. Though he saw now his nemesis was young, he didn't know whether to adopt an aggressive or submissive stance; settled for neither. Just waited.

"Lost anything?"

"Who are you?"

"Like you don't know, or haven't guessed."

"Adam Hammett."

"The very same."

"You know...I didn't kill your sister." The lack of response was unnerving, and he felt the need to continue; fill the silence. "She was angry; wanted them back. I said no. She'd been willing enough. She was..."

"A bit of a slut." Hammett finished for him.

"I never said that."

"No, I did."

"I don't think she was. I think she wanted to be, but then realised it had all gone a bit too far."

Hammett put his hands into his jacket pockets. Was his tormentor reaching for something? He tensed, but the lad – that was all he was – just seemed to be getting comfortable. When the boy spoke though, there was nothing relaxed about him. "I think you should know, although the files on your disks have passwords, a guy like me, one with obsessive behaviours, was never going to find it difficult to work out them out. Likewise that snazzy laptop."

"I wasn't going to do anything with the pictures; never have done. You've seen – they go back years. They're just my…" he hesitated, "…my obsession. Surely you can understand that."

"She was so young!" Hammett's eyes blazed, his voice more menacing for being a whisper. "It doesn't matter what a tart she was; the duty of care was with you. How old are you?"

He didn't answer. Giving his age in reply would have felt ridiculous. "I'm sorry – truly I am. Look, the prospect of getting caught scared me so much, I've changed." He hated the pleading tone in his voice, but any port in a storm. "I've given up."

"Become tit-total, eh?" Hammett's smile was chilling, the more so for him being a teenager. Like sister, like brother. In a random moment of objectivity, it seemed as inappropriate as a priest wearing one of those Guy Fawkes masks. "If that urge is in you, that drive, you can't just stop. As you said, who should understand that if not me? Besides, I saw it for myself in the way you watch women, even now, once you felt the coast was clear."

"But really, I didn't kill her."

"Who did?"

"She got angry and tried forcing my hand; said she would tell people I'd forced her to have sex."

"And did you?"

"She needed no forcing." It was out before he could stop himself. Impossible though it seemed, he had probably just made things worse. He looked around, wondering, for a moment, whether he was somehow being set up, but dismissed the idea. They stared at each other. He decided to push on. "She headed for that taped-off bit of the cliff-top. I tried to pull her back, but she tore at my arm, so violently my watch even came adrift. I started to panic. She threatened to jump if I didn't give her the pictures. The next thing I know, she's slipped – at least I assume she did." He pointed at Hammett. "You saw me hurrying away. I wanted to get as far away from the scene as possible; knew that the very thing you think now would be in everyone's minds." He breathed in deeply a couple of times. "I still don't know how and why I wasn't called into the line-up. I heard you saw me."

"Strange though it might sound, it was your lucky day. I…was distracted. In looking for Anna, I didn't pay as much attention as I should to you. While I was sure later that you had harmed her, I knew I couldn't be as positive when it came to identifying you."

There was a light-bulb moment and he gestured towards himself. "The rust-coloured shirt! That's why you needed me to wear it tonight. When I heard the police were looking for a guy with that colour shirt, I was tempted to chuck it in a skip or something, but then I couldn't sure there wouldn't be some evidence on it; some DNA or that sort of thing. Burning it might have been an option, but it would have been just my luck – Murphy's Law – that someone would have seen me and that would have been damning. But no-one came looking."

They were both lost in thought for a moment; perhaps taken back four years.

Hammett broke the silence. "Anyway, I know I said it was your lucky day back then, but that's not really the case now."

"What do you mean?" He felt a chill.

"Well, one way or the other, you still have blood on your hands, but more importantly, you felt you got away with it and kept the pictures. They are now the albatross around your neck."

He didn't know what to say to that, but knew there was more coming and just waited.

"Oh, and by the way, thank you for confirming there are pictures on the disks and laptop. I guessed there might be, but again, you were careless. I don't know whether you have other copies, but your anxiety about the ones I have has told me all I need to know. And besides, I meant it earlier; I will find your password sooner rather than later."

He wanted to curl into a ball. Nothing in his life had filled him with such self-loathing as his stupidity.

Hammett continued: "So here's what's going to happen. I'll keep them."

"Keep them? But that means anybody could..."

"Exactly! They'll be out there somewhere; in a place over which you have no control – and you'll never know when they might resurface. I want them to hang over your head like a Sword of Damocles; overshadow your life, just as the destructiveness of my sister and the destruction of my family hangs over mine. I will make it my life's work to hunt down people like you and administer justice, in whatever way is appropriate." He pointed. "And you will never know if or when the debt you owe will come up for payment. In the meantime, I think you'll suffer enough."

With that, Hammett turned to go.

"I should kill you now."

His tormentor turned to look at him for a moment. "Perhaps you should. You might be saving me a life of misery. On the other hand, those disks may then fall all the sooner into the wrong hands – the right hands, depending on your point of view." He paused as if reflecting. "Besides, I don't think even you would want the death of both siblings on whatever remnants of a conscience you have." Hammett waved, just as he had when Jack Geddis had looked out from his window. "Goodbye."

Geddis stood and watched Hammett's figure disappear down the road. He lost track of how long he stood there, once again a ghost in the world that rushed by him.

Adam Hammett, meanwhile, felt more alive than at any point he could remember in his life. For four years he had wondered whether this day would come, how it might pan out. And now, when it had come to the actual performance, the awkward sixteen year old had played it out with a mastery and calmness beyond both his years and the many products of his imagination. Perhaps there was hope for the future after all. He could be whoever he chose to be, not restricted by the constraints he had always assumed being Adam Hammett would place upon him. On this day an entirely different creature had emerged, butterfly-like; a person, perhaps, who could pay Adam Hammett's debts and some more besides.

Twenty-three years later

Then the door opened and an archetypal prison screw – peaked cap pulled low over his eyes, showing his army background, and *Donna* tattooed on his forearm – led in the prisoner. The number 71833 wasn't visible anywhere, though Logan had memorised it as he might any distinctive feature, but his observational mechanisms were not required now. This was a meeting outside the usual visiting times, by special request.

Seeing the identity of his visitor, Geddis' mouth twisted into what could only be described as a smile of pain. He was ushered by the wordless screw towards the seat.

"Well, well; DCI Dipshit – or whatever name you go by now, Hammett."

Logan leaned back in his chair and likewise gave a smile reflecting little warmth. "Better be nice to me, Jacky-boy. Remember, you ain't out of here yet." In a moment of dislocation, he noticed how he had slipped into the police patois habit with such ease. Officers did it to create the familiarity that might just ease them into the perp's confidence. It suggested, also, that they were just as streetwise and therefore would sniff out the lies. None of that was needed here; they had history – as dirty and dark as the prison in which they sat. "Don't you wish you could have left your past behind as easily as me, just by changing your name?

The two men stared at each other, as if the glass was a mirror. Is he thinking the same as me, wondered Logan; that this glass might be the only difference between us?

He wouldn't be wrong. Logan's conscience was as stained as the other man's and with dirt that would never wash out. For a man like him, it never mattered how hard you scrubbed. So the dirt had got there by other means, partly by ambition in various guises, but perhaps the only difference between his reflection and that of Geddis was the way the mirror had cracked.

On with the mask again; the one behind which he was actually a good copper, in the sense of one who got things done: "For an IT consultant you're looking quite well. Smart uniform; shaved. Discipline and early nights must be doing you good. Except for those bags under your eyes. Is it the dreams that are keeping you awake; or just the images of naïve schoolgirls that help you jerk off?" Geddis looked to the floor and Logan leaned forward, keeping his voice down: "It is to my eternal shame that I allowed you to breathe the oxygen of freedom for so long. Now, another few hours and you're out once more."

Geddis looked up again, his lip curling into a sneer, while his blue eyes seemed almost washed out as he peered through the fringe that had fallen across them. "Yeah, to what? Sex offenders register?"

Logan shrugged. He had to admit, he was enjoying this, despite having to share a space with a weasel who made his skin crawl. "Look on the bright side, Jacky-boy; firstly, you never actually raped her – just shot your load over her a couple of times."

"I never touched her at all," spat the prisoner.

Logan pursed his lips, considering these words. "True – though who knows – but a minor point." He reached into the inner pocket of his jacket and then opened his palm to reveal a memory stick, before allowing it to drop back into the pocket. "Picked it up from home before I came over. I moved your filthy catalogue into a new residence. Just a little aide memoir for you."

"You said you'd destroy it," hissed Geddis, looking over his shoulder at no-one in particular.

"C'mon, Jack, you're not a fuckwit. It's better here than on your hard drive. But it's unmarked and safe in my care; just an insurance policy in case you don't follow my instructions." Logan leaned in further still, making sure their continued conversation remained out of earshot of the screw. "You know the moral code that exists even within the criminal fraternity; news of your peccadillos gets out and the 'pecker' part of peccadillo won't be with you much longer."

Geddis slapped his hand on the table. Then, it was almost as if he sensed the warder shift, remembered himself and calmed down. He looked back at Logan and shook his head. "I knew it;" he whispered, "knew I shouldn't have believed you. This is going to hang over my head forever." He leaned back in his chair.

Logan continued the apparent see-saw by leaning forward again, this time with ferocious intent in his eyes. "And so it should, you sick fuck. Listen to you whining. I don't know whether my sister's death has haunted you, but it lives with me constantly. Actually, you should be kissing my arse." He patted his breast pocket. "With the stuff I found on your computer, you'd have been banged up in here, actually somewhere much worse, for a lot longer. When I was talking to you outside your flat, I didn't know the full range of your talents. You were pretty cocky, not encrypting your system. Maybe back then, you thought most people didn't have the technological wherewithal to even crack your passwords. Anyway, I doubt if your reception here would have been restricted to being sodomised in the showers. Instead, you probably impressed some of your prison buddies when they found out why you got sentenced; the tale of how you wanked all over this beautiful woman. I doubt the stuff about underage girls…"

"I never…!"

Logan ignored the interruption. "…would have gone down so well." He looked around the walls. "There's a strange code of honour in these places. And when you get out, at least you won't go onto a paedophile register."

"I told you, I haven't touched any kids," hissed Geddis.

Logan fought the rage. "Tell that to my dead sister – and remember, what you had them doing wasn't right, even if they were just the right side of sixteen… not that I think you could tell, because I certainly couldn't."

Geddis knew he shouldn't say anything, but he couldn't help himself. "I promise, I didn't have to force her to do anything. She was the one making suggestions."

"Oh well, that's fine then." Logan's words weren't so much laced with sarcasm as soused in it. "Next thing you'll be telling me you were doing some research; how you were abused as a child." Logan scraped back his chair. "Well then, I guess there's no point in carrying on this conversation."

Geddis raised his hands. "Wait, wait!" The screw had started to step forward, but Logan indicated things were under control and took his seat again. "What do you want me to do?"

"Well, rot in hell for starters, but I guess that'll come in due course. For now – forever in fact – what I want you to do is quite simple; stay away from Claire."

"Claire?" Geddis's frown ironed out. "Oh, my alleged victim." The frown returned. "Now why the hell would I go anywhere near her, even supposing I'd touched her…which I didn't? I don't want to end up back inside." For a moment the washed-out eyes became distant. "You've no idea what it's like in here."

"Funnily enough I have, but only from this side of the glass," he pointed to where Geddis was sitting, "and I've been making sure I'll never find out from that side for a lot longer than you've spent in here." Seeing Geddis' eyes narrow, he regretted the words as soon as they were out. Echoes of the thoughts that had filled his head during that B-road journey over the moor from Hampshire to Cornwall all those years before had wormed their way out and done so in front of a dangerous opponent. Now Geddis' features creased into a leer. "Is that it? Was this entire thing…?" There was a flame of hopeful hatred shining in Geddis' eyes as his mind worked. "I've had what's felt like a fucking eternity of time in here to think about how this whole thing evolved. So I was a fall guy, but for who? …because when you got me locked up in here, whoever did that nasty, nasty thing got to walk free. I thought maybe it was just fussy DCI Dipshit collecting brownie points by keeping his conviction record nice and pristine when he couldn't find the actual criminal, but what if it was more than that? You seem just a little too keen on this 'Claire', maybe a touch obsessed, maybe obsessed enough to grab yourself a little stolen pussy on a dark road at night knowing you had poor little me to send here in your place; a get out of jail free card. Oh they'd have a special welcome for you in here alright."

Geddis shook his head, gave an incredulous, yet mirthless laugh. "Fuck! Was it you? Am I serving time to keep you out of jail?"

Now it was Logan's turn to shake his head. "Perhaps you are a fuckwit after all. You're only serving time to pay a debt I promised long ago I would make you pay. As for Claire Treloggan, I only met her after I was assigned to the case."

The latter was a hard fact and with that, Logan felt himself regain control. He forced himself to stop twisting the signet ring. This place, its aura, had got way too far under his skin. Best to crack on and get away without any further carelessness.

Geddis looked hard at him. "Yeah, well we've only got your word for that – and we know what your word is worth."

There was ice in Logan's soul; the other man must have felt its chill, because Logan could see he regretted his comments. "You'd better trust in my word. And to make sure that you do, I'm even going to do you a favour." *Die* might have been the word that crossed Geddis' mind, but Logan could see he thought better of expressing it. "You know your life's not going to be worth living in this country as a convicted sex offender, yet you know you're never going to get away from here. Other countries wouldn't accept a man with your record. But I'm going to give you a shot at redemption; I don't want you anywhere with easy prey for your predilections, don't want that on my conscience, but I'll make sure that record comes up clean in a few, select countries where your stay in this prison would seem like a five-star hotel if you're ever caught getting up to your old tricks. Decoding your laptop taught me a lot; gave me a taste of using technology for good and bad, and I've got a lot better at it since then. Just lie low for a while. I won't be able to do it immediately, but when the fuss has died down I'll let you know. And then you'll have one month to fly away to whichever of those countries takes your fancy, maybe find a young bride who likes your money enough to make it worth being with you and settle down. I know there's no stopping people like you, and I'd have made your five years fifty if I could – but then that's the nature of plea bargains, isn't it?"

"Well, why didn't you try to fuck me over while I was in here? You've shown you're bent enough to arrange something like that."

"Because I knew it would have broken you," Logan stared at the wall, seeing a place he didn't care to visit, "and I didn't want that particular can of worms opened. A broken man doesn't care anymore." Now he leaned even closer to the window, his tone taking on a conspiratorial edge. "Look, you had to pay for your sins and this case needed a solution. Keep your mouth shut and you can still make a life somewhere. Claire…the victim gets some sort of closure. It's justice…of a sort; the best I can manage."

"Doesn't this leave her exactly where she was; a victim – just another sort?"

Now Logan pushed back his chair before continuing. "Just remember; once I give you the signal, you'd better be out of the country in a month."

He headed for the door.

"Hey," said Geddis. Logan turned. "I hope she's worth it – the damnation of your soul."

Logan snorted in derision, glanced at the screw, and then back at Geddis while patting the pocket containing the memory stick. "I hope they're worth the nightmares and the damnation of yours." He made his way back to the glass. "And it's not just Claire you'd better stay away from. There are the cheque-book journalists – in case you're thinking they might start an investigation into police corruption. I think they would find other places to dig once a copy of a certain memory stick landed on their desks. What price your freedom, eh Jacky-boy?"

Geddis bore the look of a beaten dog. "You know, Hammett, you seem mad about this woman. Doesn't it bother you that her real attacker is still out there?"

Logan didn't hesitate. He shook his head. "No. I'm there to protect her now and as far as she's concerned this guy's just an impotent pervert with issues, who can only get it up with helpless, non-consenting females." He stopped for a moment to consider. "He hasn't repeated it in six years. He had a need – a thirst; he quenched it. No, he's gone, from my patch at least."

"It doesn't worry you that he might do it again to someone else?"

Logan ignored him, nodded to the screw and made his way from the room.

Afterwards, in his car, Logan reflected on the tabloid feeding frenzy that would ensue if any of this ever got out. When the most positive part was that the police got a conviction despite knowing nothing, it gave you some measure of what the headlines might be. If they found out that a senior police officer extorted a false confession…he squeezed his eyes shut, refusing that thought the chance to materialise!

Whatever the truth of Richard's death, there was simply no evidence for anyone to get their teeth into enough to seriously question it being treated as accidental, but everything else was a collection of lies with a veneer of smoke and mirrors. Only Logan knew that Geddis had served someone else's term, but that would soon be history. No-one on the force, certainly no-one who valued their career, had any reason to poke around in this case. Police find evidence, evidence produces suspect, suspect confesses, suspect convicted, time served – end of story. He knew plenty about the sender of the mysterious letters and so hadn't even bothered asking Geddis about that; the answer lay a lot closer to home. Otherwise, all they had was a whole lot of nothing – and nothing suited him fine, because that same nothing stood between him and his goals.

****

As he settled down in the car that evening outside Claire's front door, knowing there couldn't be another letter that night – wondering, indeed, whether to plant one to drive her once and for all into his arms – Logan pondered the contradiction that he had become. He looked at his eyes in the rear-view mirror and the irony struck him; usually the prosopagnosia prevented him from recognising them, but even without that, he felt he would have struggled to know the man he was becoming; someone breaking more and more rules in an increasingly desperate bid to maintain control. The thing he'd felt hurtling along unfettered behind him that morning might have been his new self, though he sensed it was something far more dangerous.

He looked out through the steady drizzle at Claire's house, once the representation of upward mobility and achievement for Richard, now a valedictory to a dead man. It was also a symbol of Logan's uncertainties and perhaps his carelessness. He shouldn't have been here alone, defying all protocols. It was madness.

Was madness love? Was love just sex with consequences? Did the person who attacked Claire believe, perhaps for one insane moment, maybe when he first set eyes on her, that he was in love? What about Geddis and his desire for Anna?

He reeled his thoughts back swiftly inside the car, where things were safer. In here he had some control again; a place where a small set of controls defined one's interaction with the world; out of the rain in which it seemed the demons were dancing tonight.

Through the mist of his thoughts and the condensation on the windscreen, he hadn't noticed the front door open, so the tap on the car window made him almost leap out of his seat.

The rain had grown heavier and she was holding a coat over her head, from beneath which she beckoned. Logan felt safe in assuming this wasn't one of the dancing demons. He pointed to his chest and gave a questioning expression – *you mean me?* She pulled a comical face in return, which said *no, the other person in your empty car.* He signalled that he would be just a minute and she retreated indoors.

At last, having ensured the rear-view mirror framed the back window symmetrically, he got out and headed towards the house, fighting, without success, to avoid unlocking and relocking the car twice. He was grateful that particular minor fixation seemed only to apply to his car, as the remote made it a much simpler task.

17

As if everything that had been happening drew him to it, Freddy pulled out his copy of the folder containing the psychological profile of Claire's attacker. He just knew – sensed – the whole chain of events was connected to that one incident. It seemed a series of distorted ley-lines were insisting on conjoining. It wasn't difficult to tie in Claire's new-found, steely cold edge with the sudden, shocking return of the memories; the terrible ordeal in the woods now feeling like it happened only yesterday. Add to this Cissie's nightmares, Richard's tragic end – which was all over the local papers – and Ben Logan's assignment to that case too; all of it seemed part of a plan, but at the moment that plan was nothing more than a looming shape in the fog. Freddy believed re-reading the file might bring enough of a breeze to stir away the mists.

Richard's tragic end. Was that truly how he viewed it? He had to be brutally honest with himself; how could any psychologist look in the mirror and consider himself fit for duty otherwise? If he had believed Claire was deeply in love with Richard, then from that perspective he could have allowed the epithet of tragedy – so that was a blank right there! From his own point of view, he had never been a fan of the guy, the rugger-bugger type into whose arms had bounced the woman for whom Freddy had carried, if not a torch, then at least a flashlight app. She'd been in love with another man who had broken her young heart and, on the rebound, there was Richard, undeniably a charmer and charismatic with the confidence that oozed through from privilege.

And what about Jack Geddis? That was the weird part. It was as if he didn't fit into this overall picture. Okay, anyone might be capable of an act of sexual perversion, but the letters; why? He'd been someone who'd chosen to stay in the shadows – hiding his face from Claire in the car; putting a sack over her head; running away; burning any evidence of his presence in the car. She said he thanked her at the end, as if, as far as he was concerned, the act was complete; his own interactive version of a porn channel. Why would he have confessed, and why choose now to draw attention to himself and his imminent release from prison by trying to scare the living daylights out of his victim? It made no sense. Add to all of this the lack of anything in his behavioural history. There had been no real prior form; sitting near a school in your car might have suggested some bad intent, but there was nothing post-attack to suggest recidivism. In fact *impulsive* suited better than *compulsive*. It appeared to have been a one-off crime; there was not the calculation, the reptilian patience so typical of repeat sexual offenders. He'd said he'd seen Claire re-entering the clinic and had spotted his opportunity, waiting in the darkness of her car for her. Were those the actions of someone who had planned things? Even if, as per Claire's flashback, he would had to have had the cable ties, sack and a mask with him, these were things a car enthusiast might well have kept in the boot of his car; the sack could have been a hessian shopping bag, the mask something he wore to keep grease out of his hair when working under the car. There had been contradiction after contradiction in the motivations behind the crime. If you see someone and their beauty drives you crazy, would it still be a typical response to kidnap them? Maybe in a sick mind...

But for all that Geddis' story seemed to provide enough of an answer to all the practical questions, it somehow felt as though it had been concocted to do exactly that, and Freddy couldn't get away from the feeling that the attack was much more premeditated; that if Claire had remembered to lock the car then the attacker would have had a key with which to unlock it.

Richard?

Freddy had to almost shake his head to rid it of the recurring negativity about the not so dear departed husband. It had no place here...did it? Or if it did, then why? Perhaps the attacker was someone who knew Claire's husband?

Freddy pondered the strangeness of this latest unexpected train of thought – now why would he consider an acquaintance of Richard a more likely attacker than someone who knew Claire? Either way, that someone had access to their home and lives, but was it more likely to be someone connected to Richard because, white-collar high-achiever though he was, the man seemed a bully; had always exuded an aura of latent brutality, perhaps even violence. Yes, that had to be why Freddy's subconscious mind wouldn't let go; why Richard's ghost was playing at Banquo.

But the bottom line was that Geddis just didn't fit the profile. Also, the police had found nothing at all damning on his computer; normally that trove of all sins.

Or, rather, DCI Ben Logan had said they found nothing. Suddenly the thought crossed Freddy's mind; what might be found on Logan's metaphorical hard drive? In fact who was DCI Ben Logan? Strangely, Freddy had still never met him.

He remembered now the words of Inspector Heath, who had brought over the police files, so Freddy could read them through before starting his own profiling of the attacker. Logan had phoned earlier that morning, introducing himself and asking whether Freddy would be prepared to help; saying that he realised it was a bit irregular and out of left field, but Claire had insisted he was the only psychologist she would trust. Of course that had been flattering, but the whole time there had been a discordant note, not helped by Freddy knowing nothing about the new man heading up the case. Unable to nail it down, Freddy had asked Heath about Logan.

"There's nothing to tell," Heath had said, *"and I mean nothing. None of us knows why he was transferred, save that DCI Rawlings in Winchester speaks very highly of him."* He had paused, very obviously considering whether it was wise to continue before doing so. *"Bit of a cold fish. Tries to be a team player on the surface of it, but you sense, if he could walk past you in the corridor without acknowledging you he would. I take great pleasure in always saying good morning and then there's this exaggerated friendly greeting. I wish I could pretend I like him, but I don't warm to him."*

****

It was as if Logan had walked through some sort of magic portal instead of a front door, into a kingdom of wildness and beauty, encapsulated in this woman. She was even more than he'd imagined in his fantasies; so beautiful; so beautiful – a beauty refreshed for him every time he saw her. Perhaps the one favour bestowed on him by his condition was that he saw her effectively for the first time every time they met. And now that they were alone, the curtain, whether iron, velvet or ice, had fallen away, and he was thankful to find beyond it the appetites of a whore.

At times during that feverish night he felt them drifting apart; she to the place where ghosts, as well as men, were laid; he to the dark pit where his own monsters were enslaved. From the moment he had entered her world he'd become a creature of sensations. They were free spirits in that house, revisiting all his fantasies on the stairs, the dining table, the lounge floor and, at last, on the bed itself. No single word of love was exchanged, uttered nor demanded.

Anyway, what was love? Just strange shapes formed by cooling lava when you'd finished dancing on the rim of the crater. As another eruption built and he looked down at her, he could not have cared less if he had toppled over the edge and been consumed by the ferocious heat.

When exhaustion finally overtook him, his last memory of his old life was her dismounting him, leaving him softening and cooling in the night air, aware that everything which had gone before – the sighs, the heartache, the sleeplessness, the hatred, both hers and his – distilled to that flaccid piece of flesh; his need to put it inside her and her need to accept that it still drove a part of her. He knew, beyond that, that they mistrusted each other, but for very different reasons.

She collapsed with a groan next to him on the bed, threw an arm across his chest, and that was where he found her in the morning.

At which point, he just about managed to stop himself sitting bolt upright. He liked to believe he thought deeply about life, too deeply if his pathology was anything to go by, so how had this simplest of revelations escaped him till now, unless he had been avoiding it. He was drawn to damaged women. Whether he saw them as a suitable, understanding partner, or whether saving them was a way of saving himself…perhaps that was a thought too far for the moment.

But there was no denying the premise. The way he found Claire Treloggan at her loveliest when she looked troubled and tired. How disturbed he had felt a few years back by the inappropriate thoughts crossing his mind during that final case in Hampshire, from which the move to Cornwall had provided escape, not just career advancement. Was he somehow compensating for fleeing home when his mother's strength finally ran out and her alcoholism rendered her a stranger? He had never returned. He doubted he ever would.

Was this why, amongst all the random facts one could choose to remember, he had never forgotten the word Kintsugi, a method used by the Japanese for repairing broken ceramics in which they created a lacquer often mixed with gold? For them, the damage was part of the history of a piece, part of its charm and this was their way of recognising that, rather than hiding it.

Turning his head to the left, he looked long at Claire, whose peaceful features bore no hint of a disturbed sleep nor her recent troubles. Hard to believe she was damaged goods. He puffed out his cheeks – thank God for that!

And true to his own peccadilloes, she had left him feeling dirty, or rather his own needs had done so and he needed to shower.

****

She felt him stirring; clung tight so that he couldn't move and looked up at him with a smile.

During the night, Claire, too, had felt how one tiny push might have sent their coupling bodies tumbling. The primitive level of their physical desire had amazed her. At times, she had wanted to surrender her mind to the darkness as well as her body, but she couldn't afford to; not if her plan was to succeed.

There had been one key moment – an acid test. She had reached across to take Logan's tie from the neat pile of his clothes. As she had offered him her wrists for bondage, she had looked into his eyes and seen the truth, indeed the proof of whether their union could ever have lasted; the mark of whether it was forged in heaven or in two personal versions of hell. His uncertain desire flared before guttering and she knew he was her man. The conviction had been growing; now there could be no doubt. Because of what that meant – and despite her worst fears – there was no mistaking the thrill it gave her.

****

"I ache," she said, her words groggy.

"Quelle surprise." He grinned. She felt him try to get up and held him fast.

"Hey, I've got to report back… and I need a pee."

She had to think fast. Looking down, she saw the bulge and whipped back the duvet to reveal it. "Well, you're not aiming that at my toilet bowl in its current state".

With that, her mouth was on him. She saw his toes curling. Beyond them and the end of the bed, she took in his neat clothes, which he had insisted on folding, despite the urgency of their sex. There were things about Logan she needed to know, and it meant being out of the house for a while before he left today.

Gentle, provocative, she lapped at him. "Stay for breakfast."

He groaned. "I can't."

She started running her tongue the length of him. Wherever this darkness of purpose and desire had emerged from, she welcomed it now. Though it seemed a simplistic point of view, she guessed the beautiful beast had lurked within her all her life; more shocking was to contemplate what exactly had stirred it from its slumber. Not Ben Logan; he was just a victim or beneficiary of it, depending on your point of view. Her mind returned once more, just for a moment, to a clearing in the woods where, hands and feet bound, her breath dampening the inside of a hessian sack, she had felt the power of the beast in the raging of the wind and the silence of a man driven to the edge of madness by it.

She looked up at Logan, past his weapon and his weakness; her eyes taunted him. "Your men will cover for you." She shifted position, made a provocative cupping gesture on her breasts. "You can say I had a…disturbed night, and you had to take care of me."

With that she plunged her mouth over him again.

As Logan lay recovering from his morning delight, Claire got ahead of him into the bathroom and did not allow him in until she was made up and all set to go. As soon as she heard him running the shower she set to work, knowing exactly where to find the things she needed.

"I'm just going to pop over to my mother and check on Cissie. I'll be back as quickly as I can," she called through the bathroom door. "Then we can breakfast or whatever you want." It was hard putting the lascivious note into her voice when her mind was on other things.

She was pretty confident that Logan was someone who would take a long time to get ready. A glance at her watch as she drove away; 08.40 – an hour would be enough. Cissie would be fine at her mother's. Claire had other things to do.

As she left the grounds, the policemen in the car looked at her and she pulled alongside, jerking a thumb over her shoulder towards the house.

"He needed the bathroom and I've let him use the shower as well after a night in the car."

The one she knew as Detective Inspector Heath raised his eyebrows. "Alright for some." He smiled, though it seemed forced. "If only all witnesses were so accommodating, ma'am." He gestured towards his colleague in the car. "Some of us saw the sunrise to the accompaniment of snoring and the aroma of fast food."

She gave Heath a cheery wave and headed off.

"We've been in the car all night too ...and I was only resting my eyes," said Donaldson as he watched her car depart. He tapped one of the burger cartons. "Bet melted cheese isn't the only thing he's washing off this morning."

"Yup. Probably dined at the Y." Heath grinned, but Donaldson could tell by the way he glanced towards the house, the Inspector's mind was racing.

"Wonder if he went large."

There was no reaction for a moment, but then Heath did throw his head back and burst out laughing.

As the crow flew it wasn't far to 17 Forest Avenue. Haring along the country roads felt different now in her Volvo S60. The car was nimble, responsive, but more importantly, unlike years back, she had not only purpose and focus – she had control. In fifteen minutes she had reached her destination in Truro – some might have said destiny.

She parked up round the block, ensured that all of her distinctive auburn hair was hidden beneath a woolly hat, and then pulled on the shapeless, brown jacket that she had picked up in the British Heart Foundation shop. Next, on went two extra pairs of walking socks and the pair of size 7 trainers – two sizes too big. Everywhere the ground was wet; if she did happen to leave a footprint it wasn't going to be traced back to her. From the car's ashtray she produced the little plastic bag containing cigarette butts from outside the local pub. Things she had heard during chats with Logan would now be used to mislead him; if it came down to forensics, it wasn't going to be Claire who had entered his flat. And if what she suspected about him was true, getting away with this visit without leaving a trace would be nigh-on impossible, so she might as well leave the smell of red herrings.

Hat turned down, coat-collar turned up, in anonymous jeans and old Nike trainers, she made her way round the block to the flats, her sweating hand clasped tightly around the spare key she had taken from his wallet. She took the stairs to the second floor; people passed on stairs – no time to stand and study you like in a lift. Also, it gave her a chance to pull on the plastic gloves.

As she stood outside Flat 17, her heart thumped on the doors of all the neighbouring apartments, but her nerve held and after a moment's stiffness when it seemed the key wouldn't turn, there was give and a click.

And then she was in.

As she took in the scene, another voice screamed: *"Alien alert!"* But while she might have been a stranger on Planet Logan, she asked herself whether he, too, wasn't from outer space.

"Whoa!" It was more of a voiced breath than a word. "There's minimalist – and then there's this."

When she had pictured this moment, two details had been different. First, although she had suspected Logan had compulsive tendencies, she had put them down to nerves and imagined that his apartment would still look as if it had been lived in. Second, she had assumed she would be in a panic of haste. Instead she was fascinated and needed to take a closer look, even though first impressions had, in all probability told her all she needed to know.

Her task would either be very easy or impossible – she suspected the latter.

At last, she was able to defy gravity and move across the planet surface. Her training shoes didn't appear to have left a mark on the spotless, laminated floor, but with the technology available these days she suspected a bold footprint would become visible under some sort of ultra-violet light. That didn't matter, as long as Logan didn't spot it straight away, though even a speck of dust or a hair would almost rampage with roaring intent across this sterility.

Set dead square in the centre of the lounge was one table and a solitary, matching chair – it seemed visitors were not welcome in this theme park. "At least the queues would be short in Loganworld," she muttered; both the words and the sound of the nervous giggle that followed made her realise how close she was to hysteria.

There was only one bookcase, but the contents suggested he was well read. Still, one shelf was filled with identically-bound Reader's Digest condensed books, placed in a specific repeat pattern of colours; red, brown, green, red, brown, green. In a corner hung a plasma screen above a sound bar and a subwoofer; no cluttering CDs needed, just Bluetooth and a phone. These items would have been unremarkable except for the complete lack of any dust on the shiny black surfaces. There was a DVD player, but no sign of any discs. The walls were devoid of pictures. Nowhere were there any photographs. On the mantelpiece of the mock fireplace stood a faux street sign bearing the legend: *If you are tired of London, you are tired of life.* At first, relief flooded through Claire; this was a literal sign of identity – finally, a sense of belonging; the only one, but something nagged at her. At last she got it; this apparent touch of eccentricity in an otherwise barren place felt less like a statement than a scream; a desperate attempt to be normal in a life that felt anything but? Yet it had misfired; the words of Dr Samuel Johnson were famous enough for her to know that they had been misquoted. Besides that, she knew Logan was not from London.

She could hazard an educated guess at what she would find in the kitchen and almost didn't bother with it. There were identical jars – labels aligned with geometric precision – and utensils, which might as well have been compass needles pointing out magnetic north, such was the exactitude with which they'd been put away.

"God oh God oh God!" said Claire to herself, whispering despite everything; knowing the silence accused her. Part of her felt sorry for Logan, for the burden he carried every day – the fight to appear normal. She knew well enough what a struggle that could be, but at least it was because of events and, to an extent, you could react to those; try your best to shape them. For Logan, life was a battle against an unseen enemy – your genes.

Enough! This wasn't helping her; guilt would be her own invisible foe if she wasn't careful, distracting her from the very course of action she had just referenced; shaping her destiny. She had things to do.

The bedroom contained a futon, one unit of drawers devoid of any decoration, a wardrobe and a digital clock. *Precision…everywhere precision.* A small mirror hung on the wall, placed, it occurred to her, where it would be of zero use. It seemed to have some sort of sticker on it. She wandered over and read: "If you're looking handsome here, remember you're the opposite." She smiled at the apparent humour, till the sadness in that interpretation struck her.

Again – enough!

Turning away, she took in the scene.

"Ben Logan, you should have joined the army – except you might have ended up killing any other squaddie whose kit wasn't laid out correctly." She puffed out her cheeks and then shuddered with understanding. "Boy, it's no wonder you fucked me into kingdom come – pardon the pun." She went to run her hand over the futon cover, but withdrew it. "I doubt any of the surfaces in *this* place have had cum stains visited on them." She reconsidered. "I doubt they've had visitors; full stop." Claire shuddered again; what sad, caged animal had she unleashed under her own roof?

She opened a drawer, hoping to find some trace of humanity, and was startled, though for no good reason, to find a notebook. Perhaps it was the apparent age of the book. No-one, no matter how obsessive, could prevent the pages of a book from reflecting its age, unless they kept it hermetically sealed so moisture couldn't get at them. This book was clearly special and, she just sensed somehow, loved.

Thus, it was with an element of shame at her intrusion that she picked it up and opened it.

What she found both fascinated and confused her. She realised she had been expecting a diary and in many ways she assumed that was what it was, in the sense that it had dates. However, the first one was, by her calculation, thirty years before.

She flicked through and noted how the writing developed from that of a child into an adult. For a moment, she felt a little squeamish and dishonest in doing so. Such sensitivity was, under the circumstances, a paradox and perhaps hypocritical, but it was the child's handwriting that gave her pause; poking her nose into an adult's secret life was one thing, but eavesdropping on the inno-cence of disturbed child another. Then she thought of Cissie and the decision to continue was easier. Logan's past was exactly that; hopefully, in a way yet to be fully revealed, her actions might safe-guard her daughter's future. The path ahead was unclear, but she was on it now and had to continue.

Perhaps *directory* or *catalogue* might have been a better description of the book's contents. She thought for a distracted moment about Logan's extremely neat police notebook. There seemed to be a succession of names, none of which meant anything to her, followed in each case by some sort of physical description; an odd one, usually consisting of a handful of identifiers – that word came to her because there appeared to be no facial features. In one instance a large mole was mentioned, in another thinning hair; here a scar, there a patch on a pair of jeans. Hair colour and style, about which Logan seemed to know more than most hairdressers, was always there unless, as she advanced through the pages and the years, baldness was referenced.

There were also events listed, but not the likes of birthdays, holidays or sport. Here, someone had fallen off a bicycle. A page or two further on a girl called Lucy had cut her hair from its previous shoulder length to a cropped look and changed the colour from black to bleached blonde. What stood out in that instance, and everywhere else, was no sense of judgement, just a cold recording of fact.

Claire was fascinated, but also repelled. Never mind her own sense of intruding, this read like a stalker's notes. Given what had happened to her, the idea made her hands shake more than they were already.

And suddenly they trembled. A name leapt off a page at her, or rather, the page itself leapt out at her, as if it had been lurking there waiting to spring. To that point, information had been crammed into the book, as if the writer, or diarist, had meant this to be a single book to last a lifetime. The handwriting and the spelling had been gradually making a transition from childish towards its adult incarnation.

Then, perhaps a quarter of the way into the book, was a whole double page apparently devoted to just one person. In still fairly youthful writing, there was a description: *adult, dark-brown hair, scuttling gait, rust-coloured shirt with button missing from left cuff, tan-line from watch on wrist.* After that, in the more grown-up writing prevalent on later pages, came an addition: *scar on neck.* Strange how the entries that followed, stating days this character visited the Waterfront Café, seemed creepier as they suggested the mind of a stalker. There was an address added, which only fuelled that idea…

…and then all else blurred, her thoughts and the words on the page as she spotted a name, understanding now for whom that page existed, yet not understanding why as she read the words '*Jack Geddis*'!

A thousand other thoughts now filled the empty space of Logan's flat. Claire slammed the book shut. She felt her legs weaken and needed to sit on the bed. There was acid in the back of her throat and she fought hard against the nausea.

They knew each other! What the fuck! Because the book had just been starting to make sense. For whatever reason, Logan had kept a note of everyone he had ever met. She knew he had it in him to be obsessive, but…

Another thought flared and she grabbed the book again; leafed through to the date she had first met Logan.

There she was: *Claire Treloggan. Tall, auburn hair, blue eyes, small beauty spot mole to right of mouth.* There was one more word – she didn't know whether she found its presence flattering or frightening: *Beautiful.*

One certain impact of the word was that it brought her round again to the present. She closed the book, went to replace it in the drawer…and spotted what had lain beneath it –

a memory stick; startling in its unexpectedness a single fruit tempting her to take a bite. She knew time was of the essence, but there was no way she could resist. Claire picked it up with care and returned to the television. Taking excruciating note of the position from which she moved it, she picked up the remote and switched on the TV. Now she inserted the stick in a USB slot. Several features appeared and she selected one.

She wished she hadn't.

The pictures and a couple of short recordings, taken, she presumed, from the internet, made her skin crawl — left her feeling unclean — and wondering what images had flashed through Ben Logan's mind as he'd spent his lust on and in her the last night. She shuddered, trying not to imagine how her woman's body had been explored by his hands even as this perverted filth must have been running through the dark, dank alleyways of his mind.

Something else chilled her blood; they said the innocent eyes of children saw things for what they really were. Was that why Cissie always cried for her mother when Logan was around? Did she see him approaching the house and recognise him for what he was — a monster?

Oh my God! What if he was the shadow approaching from beyond the wall in the land of Nowhere?

One thought distilled from the cocktail of horrors in her mind; this bastard was going to get what was coming to him. This changed everything.

And now she wanted to be away from there; it wasn't safe, in particular if he discovered his secret was out.

Claire went to return the memory stick, but in doing so noticed other things further back in the drawer. They didn't make her feel any better about Logan, but that was a lost cause now. These, at least, were things she could use to bring him down. She stuffed the items into her coat pockets and, after a moment's contemplation, likewise pocketed the stick.

Now, in haste, and cursing herself for becoming distracted, she did what she had come there to do in the first place.

At that point she should have left, but having seen the contents of the memory stick, she was drawn once more to the book. She leafed through it, looking with fresh eyes, though perhaps horrified and anxious might have been more appropriate adjectives. How many of the listed names, particularly those of girls, might have been targets for the writer's perverted lens? Was this a catalogue detailing the results of more than one mental condition?

A particular entry caught her eye. There was no name, just a row of question marks, but...

God, no!

She was overtaken by that sudden bitter taste. Bile burnt the back of her throat; the threatening emptiness of this sick place was an emetic and she could not suppress it any longer.

She was standing with her hands on her knees – hysteria rising with the bile as she wondered what would happen if she vomited in this sterile clinic of an apartment – when she heard the key in the door.

She retained enough presence of mind – enough sense of time and place – to step out of the bedroom.

Of course, there was nowhere to hide.

18

The pain in his neck was excruciating and when he managed to straighten it at last, Freddy looked around him with distaste, noticing the empty wine glass on the table by the chair.

And then the nagging started, accompanying the pulsing headache; annoyance, irritation. Had he been on the verge of some sort of breakthrough when he'd fallen asleep? He couldn't be sure; it seemed Ariadne had withdrawn the thread.

And there it was again – the sound which must have woken him; the doorbell. He glanced at the clock.

"Shit!"

That would be Lynsey, his PA. He rushed downstairs and opened the door.

"A thousand apologies, Lynsey, I was working late."

She appraised him from top to toe. "I can see that." There was a glint in her eye. "So this is what Doctor Dessler looks like first thing in the morning." She popped her tongue in her cheek. "You know, in a way I could get used to it."

Despite his confusion and weariness Freddy saw something in Lynsey, perhaps because, for the first time, he himself was vulnerable. How had he failed to notice just how attractive she was? Perhaps it was because she was in a relationship so he'd assumed she was forbidden fruit? Had she smiled like that before? For God's sake, she must have smiled before – his was not a draconian regime – but like that? Perhaps she was no longer in that aforementioned relationship. Note to self, he thought – start looking in the right direction.

She breezed past him towards the practice rooms and then turned to him with a very appropriate face. "But, if I may, I suggest you don't allow your patients to see you like this."

He nodded. "Um, no – quite. What time's the first one today?"

"09.45. I'll fire up the Nespresso, Doctor Dessler. The usual Lungo?"

"Yes please. Thank you, Lynsey." She turned to go. "Oh and…" – she stopped and looked over her shoulder – "…call me Freddy."

"Very well, Doctor Dessler."

****

He didn't get back to the file containing the psychological profile till that night, by which time it was too late.

Of course Lynsey hadn't known what it was all about, but Freddy had been very gratified to observe that she'd had no problem chatting with him until well after hours, nor with his suggestion of ordering in a pizza. Without being too obvious – in his opinion anyway – he'd gleaned that she had split up with her partner the month before, but he had retained enough savoir faire not to ask her out on a date…yet.

After that, once she had gone home, he was a-buzz with adrenalin; unable to go to sleep; shaking his head for a fool for having missed what had been staring him in the face for so long. It seemed the lingering aroma of his desire for Claire had dulled his other senses.

And that was when he had remembered the file and, still being wide awake, had poured a glass of wine, before sitting in the same chair as the previous night in the hope of reenergising the cognitive powers.

And they had returned alright – with a vengeance.

Now he bent over the file in the spotlight of the reading lamp while the rest of the room grew darker, as his supporting cast of shadows entered stage left. He heard their whispers and musings about why the file, a copy of which he had handed to the police, remained closed in his hands. Instead he turned it over and over.

Not that the contents were unimportant, even though, or perhaps because the details bore no resemblance to the man they had nailed in the end. Indeed that had sounded the first warning bell for Freddy the previous night. He had to trust in his abilities, and they had never been that wrong before.

"Pristine," he said to anyone listening, looking at the edges of the manila folder. Never referred to as part of any discussion with the police once he had presented it to them. "As if untouched by human hands; rather like Jack Geddis' hard drive." He gazed into the darkness for a moment.

He looked away from the file and pictures formed in the night.

"I wonder," muttered Freddy. One image appeared in his mind's eye, spinning; a green, computer-generated skull on the screen of the criminal physiognomist, only it wouldn't flesh out at first.

It was a worm of curiosity that needed feeding. He may have understood the workings of that most complex machine, the brain, but computers weren't things to which he turned readily. However, he went to his laptop and searched for any articles on Jack Geddis' trial.

"If I can see you again," he muttered, standing bent over the screen, "maybe I can have a stab at understanding you."

He remembered the photo that had been in the press at the time, but only now was he dispassionate enough to look beyond Geddis' face in the foreground, at the police officers behind him who had solved the case. Freddy had to sit down.

Sit before his legs gave way. This changed everything; boy did it!

He hadn't attended the trial, due to work commitments, but also because he knew Claire would only be testifying remotely.

Besides, he had felt a need to distance himself from it all, worried his reputation might suffer if he was seen as being dangerously unprofessional. Afterwards, his sole concern had been for Claire. He had to ask himself – if he had been there, would he have picked up on this? Might he have seen little signs; nervous tics with which had he grown familiar even during the very short time he had been witness to them. How many years had it been now; fifteen or so had passed between their talk at the university and the trial? The hair was now shorter, dark, where before it had been fair, and neater – but still! How had he missed this? Were we so unobservant as human beings that, given a different name, we fail to recognise a face. Who had been suffering facial blindness in this instance!?

Now, too, he understood the discordant note in the telephone conversation; literally, a note – the tone of his voice, familiar, but different.

He remembered other things too.

Twenty-one years before

"I guess I should be going. I'm not sure how much this has helped you."

The postgrad sat up straight. "Oh, don't worry about that. This has been fascinating!" Then he seemed to remember himself. "I mean, of real relevance. I hope it has helped you. I could help you further."

"Do I need help? I seem to have got this far."

"Of course, but then you did apply to take part in this study, so I don't think…I hope I'm not jumping to conclusions when I say I believe this is not something you've shared with anybody before."

"Sharing's an interesting concept, isn't it? We all share our lives, every day, without trying. Doing it deliberately is just exhibitionism."

The postgrad's eyebrows drew together in a furrow over his nose. "Perhaps an extreme point of view, but, look, I do want to ask you a favour. A big favour. Well, not so much a favour as a…"

"And that would be?"

The postgrad took a deep breath. "I believe you suffer from what is known as prosopagnosia."

"I know."

"You know?"

"Well, I say I know; I meant I had kinda worked it out. What teenager doesn't try to understand how his body works? My sister might have been a more extreme example of that."

Sensing the postgrad's discomfort with that last statement, he pushed on. "Okay, what's the favour?"

"I would love to find out how much comes out under hypnosis. I've only read about your condition, but have never met it. It would be fascinating, for example, to know whether details, facial expressions or signals blocked out by the conscious brain surface from some subconscious part; whether faults in the occipital lobe are overridden…"

"I hate to break it to you, doc," he broke into the flow, though not without regret, "but some things are best left buried."

The postgrad tilted his head to the right and pulled a wistful expression. "A shame – but okay; absolutely, that is your prerogative." He placed his palms firmly on the arms of the chair and sighed. "There is someone else due in five minutes. I cannot hope for as compelling a session from them. Thank you."

They rose as one and made their way to the door. He held his hand out towards the postgrad. "Thank you."

"Thank you! Remember, if you ever so decide that some things bear being exhumed, just look me up. I'm…"

Hurriedly, he raised a hand. "I know, Professor Dowker …or rather his research assistant I assume. But I think this day has served its purpose; made me realise how much of my baggage could be lost just by ripping the name tag off it".

And then, as he gripped the door handle to leave, he turned and observed how the postgrad looked taken aback; assumed the latter had seen some flash of anger or mania in his eyes. "And that one last burden; I know of a crime and of a guilty man. If it takes me the rest of my life I'll ensure that there's a fitting punishment."

****

The force of the statement so stunned Freddy Dessler that by the time he had blinked to clear it the other man had gone. It was going to be hard to bring his mind back to researching the negative influence of emotions on dyadic negotiation after this!

****

"Some things are best left buried." Perhaps so, but if suppressed for too long, what might happen? Springs wound too tight for too long had a habit of snapping.

Freddy forced those shaking legs across to his desk, fired up his laptop again and googled, all the time tutting for never having looked into this.

No good berating yourself, Freddy, said the good angel on his right shoulder, *back then, it would have gone against his desire for anonymity.*

But if you hadn't been so concerned with your doctorate, you might have tried a little harder to help such an obviously troubled soul, said the bad angel on his left.

He dredged his memory banks and remembered where the girl had been washed up – Trebarwith Strand; a stunning beach with rugged cliffs which he had visited many a time. Now he focussed on the press, searching back for anything.

At last, he got lucky. The story of a girl thrown over the cliffs and washed up on that beach some way further up the coast was recorded, or rather an anniversary of the suspected killer never having been found. Her name – Anna Hammett. Her brother, Adam, had been unable to identify the suspect, despite having seen him clearly.

The words of the student came back to him: *"Spiritually I left home a long time ago. I think I might even change my name; a complete fresh start."*

So, Hammett must have followed his own advice and ripped the name tag off his baggage to become Logan, and Freddy now knew he would have to set all sentiment aside.

"Yes, the answer's in here," Freddy's eyes gleamed in the lamp-light, "even if the details are no clearer. Whether we're looking at a man with obsessive behaviour patterns or mannerisms; or simply someone with access to all the data and information that controlled the outcome of this case."

He continued to scrutinise the folder, amazed that he had not paid proper attention to its fate before. All his other hard-copy files were well-thumbed and a bit dog-eared as a result of his discussions with the people who'd requested them. If the original of this one had only been through the hands of the Detective Chief Inspector, it meant nobody else properly qualified to assess it had seen it, had seen that it pointed away from Jack Geddis.

So, what did it all signify? He needed to discuss it with someone. Pacing up and down his study, Freddy Dessler addressed the night; always a staunch ally when he needed a sounding board.

"Well, the fact is, I don't really know yet *what* it means. The possibilities are many." He stared into the dark as he circled, as if studying that green hologram again. "Is this the turning head of a man for whom each day meant the repression of his real, imperfect self, until it culminated in an explosion of semen and disgust as he contemplated the object of his desire, helpless in his hands, but unwilling; an act of pure physical release, but ultimately empty? How he must have longed to see her eyes; see some love. Yet he knew he would see only fear, so better not to see them at all.

"Or, perhaps more likely, is this someone altogether more calculating; brokering a crime, which he knew would bring him, as the local Detective Chief Inspector, a double reward; direct and prolonged contact with a beautiful woman whose misfortune it was to become his obsession the moment he walked through her door, and the chance to take revenge on the man who had, he believed, killed his sister? Did he suppress my file and if so, for what reason? Did he stop the questions it contained from being asked?"

Freddy took a large swallow of wine and looked at the file. Where Geddis seemed to be something of a nonentity, all his attentions turned inward to his own sordid compulsions, the file's contents described a highly able and ambitious man, floating through civilised society hiding his true monster, probably holding a position of power and respectability that still didn't compensate for deep seated feelings of sexual inadequacy. Had Logan recognised himself in it and decided it was too close to home to allow it to see the light of day?

No. Somehow Freddy did not believe Logan had it in him to be the perpetrator, even had he been located in the county at the time of the crime, but it had been a major risk hiding the file, an action that might lead some officers down the trail of *no smoke without fire?* Honour amongst thieves, or coppers, only went so far, and if he remembered Heath's comments correctly then Logan wouldn't have been able to count on much goodwill there.

Freddy threw himself back down in his chair and rested his elbows on his knees.

"So, why suppress the file – assuming he did? On their own, these profiles rarely resolve anything. They're usually just broad brushstrokes; sky and sea. They still need the finer details sketched in. They're proof of nothing."

And the word *nothing* prompted Freddy to think about Jack Geddis again. As he had concluded the night before, there was nothing in his past to hint at what was to come. Freddy thought of that personal computer hard drive once more, which Logan had said contained, again, nothing incriminating. Unusual, to say the least, especially for someone supposedly disturbed enough to have committed the attack on Claire. The police normally scrutinised even the most tenuous of leads. The hard drive couldn't have just been blank. What if Logan had removed anything of relevance? What if Jack Geddis was *his* blank canvas? When a man confessed with no prompting, the first thing the police did was doubt him. They would check his background; go through his files, his computers. Even if they found the man was a criminal, if his activities didn't fit the pattern, or a psychological profile cast doubt on things, they would throw out the confession. But if you were a detective also unhealthily obsessed with the victim and desperate to get a conviction, and if you had your man, by whatever means, would you do what had to be done to keep things that way?

The victim! Freddy sat up straight. That word needed redefining. Was it Claire, or did helping her then avenge Anna? Logan himself was a victim – of a condition which had mocked him years before by preventing him identifying his sister's killer. Perhaps the most salient outcome of Geddis going to jail had been catharsis for Adam Hammett.

"…a fitting punishment."

So, now something else jarred – why request the profile at all? If you had your plan and your man, why introduce potential elements of doubt? Maybe Logan was hoping the ideas in the file would back his own findings.

Or perhaps it was a smokescreen, camouflage to keep prying eyes from spotting that the evidence that had convicted Geddis was false, planted by Logan.

So Geddis, therefore, would be Logan's – Hammett's – guilty man deserving of punishment. If so that made Logan an extremely dangerous person in Freddy's eyes. If there was the remotest chance he was framing an innocent person, at least a person innocent of this crime, for the attack on Claire, then he was very dangerous indeed.

"Oh my God!"

Love might sometimes be an obsession, but obsession was never love.

Another terrible scenario had just emerged from a shadowy corner. Never mind that first crime — what if there had been another? That overwound spring, freed from its great burden, exploding into shards.

What if, whilst nailing Geddis, that dangerous mind had become obsessed with the woman who was providing the possibility for that long desired for punishment? And what if there was an obstacle in your path; driving it off that path, that clifftop, might be your only way through.

Freddy glanced at his watch; it was gone midnight — too late to risk a call when Claire and Cissie's fragile psyches might be deep in their nightly battle with their demons, but it was imperative he shared this with Claire, whether she liked it or not.

****

As it turned out, he arrived in Claire's lane later that morning just in time to see a car, which he knew wasn't Claire's pulling away from the gates. He was tempted to nip through before they closed again, but an outstretched arm from another car parked outside the gates signalled him to stop. He guessed this was the surveillance team and indeed recognised the man who got out of the car to approach him after he had pulled over.

"Excuse me, sir, may I ask…" As he wound down his window the policeman stopped in mid-sentence. "Ah, Doctor Dessler. Nice to see you." It was Inspector Heath.

"If you're after Mrs Treloggan, I'm afraid you've just missed her."

"Missed her? Was that Hamm…er…DCI Logan's car?"

"Yes, sir. But she left before him — about half an hour before, I'd say. She let him use the shower this morning, apparently. Alright for some, eh? Still, he was parked up there all last night."

I bet he was, thought Freddy. Something in the looks on the faces of the two officers suggested their thoughts echoed his. He was, however, aware in the midst of everything that the twinge was less than it might have been before pizza with Lynsey. "Oh, ok; any idea where she's gone?"

"Search me, though I would assume she's gone to check up on her daughter."

"Check up on Cissie? Is something wrong? Is she in hospital?"

"Don't think so. For the last couple of nights the little thing's been with her grandmother. Best place, if you ask me."

"Right; well, thank you."

Freddy wound up his window and sped off. There was nothing more he could say to the officers. You couldn't exactly tell them you had a bad feeling, but that was what he had and he was scared.

19

It had always struck him as one of life's ironies that his condition – for want of a better word as he had been neither examined nor analysed – should be known as a disorder, given that one of its symptoms, for him anyway, was the need for order. However you labelled it, it was a double-edged sword, giving you almost a sixth sense – perhaps real, perhaps imagined – if something was genuinely out of place in your world. So, even before he stepped through his front door, he knew someone had been in his apartment. However, in this instance he'd already worked out who, even before he had set off.

He stepped in.

It was strange; under other circumstances he would have wondered who the hell this was and might have assumed a tramp, given the shapeless clothing, the woollen hat pulled down over the hair and the shoes that were out of proportion to the legs. But not this time. The only flesh visible other than hands was the face; no use to a man suffering prosopagnosia.

"Claire. I knew you'd come." He scanned the room, needing neither his police skills nor his intuition to know that she had been everywhere.

"Ben. How…?" She broke off.

"Claire," he knew he sounded patronising, but couldn't help himself, "as you've already guessed I have certain…compulsions; why on earth did you think I wouldn't notice my spare key wasn't in my wallet?"

"Ben, I…" She shrugged. "I'm sorry. What can I say?"

Despite everything, the tears that filled her eyes touched him. "It's ok, Claire."

"You're right. I guessed there were some problems. I think, after everything that's happened to me, I…"

"…needed to check on me. Like I said, I understand." This was his chance, despite the inauspicious circumstances. He hoped his face didn't give the lie to his words – he *did* understand. After all, he had also needed to know *she* was damaged; imperfect.

He stepped forward. *Brave girl*, he thought, when she didn't take a step back. However, there was something in her eyes; you weren't a policeman for so long without noticing. He couldn't put his finger on what, for the moment.

What did leap out at him was the clothing. "Very clever," he said. "Of course, I'd have known the evidence was there to mislead me," – he looked at her coat when she tried to evince innocence – "but I admire your resourcefulness."

He realised that he was now subjecting his signet ring to a relentless twirling, but took some satisfaction from knowing that this sign of tension might well be causing her discomfort too. He wanted her to feel as edgy as him. It was something they could share, if only in its release.

Now he pointed to the chair. "Please, sit down."

He knew she wouldn't want to, so he plonked himself down on the floor and she took his lead, perching ill-at-ease on the chair.

"So," he continued, "now we know each other's imperfections…"

"Imperfections?" She gestured around the room.

"I'm not talking about our lifestyles, Claire." That was rather tiresome of her; he had expected better. "I'm talking about our states of being." He raised his eyebrows. "The sort of thing that makes me forget to offer you a drink, for example." He made to get up.

"It's ok. I don't suppose offering someone a coffee is the immediate or normal reaction on finding them uninvited in your home."

He gave a little laugh of acknowledgement, but it did not last. "Did you find what you were seeking?"

"Yes." She replied a little too readily and he noticed a hint of disingenuousness in her voice. For Logan there was a high-pitched note in the air – white noise – which might crack the tension at any moment. Their repressed calmness was almost Victorian; he knew from the position of her body that all Claire wanted to do was run. That hurt him, but he wanted this chance to turn it all around; to change everything.

"So, what were you looking for, Claire?" The eyes had it again, not their expression, which was beyond his powers to read, but the blinking pattern; something he had learned to translate as part of his coping mechanisms. He could see her edginess and hoped it was just because she had been caught out. That was what he wanted to believe – chose to – but still he couldn't eschew all bitterness. "A sign that it might have been me that took you to the woods? Or that I had something to do with Richard's disappearance?"

"No, I've never thought those things."

She might have been lying, but he preferred to believe her. "Why not?"

"Well for a start, you weren't the original detective put on the case and I was told you had just moved here."

"Okay, that takes care of the attack...but Richard's disappearance? I had motive – motivation. You knew...know I'm strongly attracted to you."

He enjoyed her very obvious discomfort with his direct questioning.

"It's never felt likely. But you're right; I sensed you had certain obsessive behaviours and before I..." she paused, tellingly, "...

committed to you I just wanted to know how much you were suppressing the problem; what exactly you were hiding from me."

"You see it as a problem?" He knew that was a petulant response, but couldn't help himself.

"No, Ben, I don't." He hoped she meant that, but where he might have breathed a huge sigh of relief, he found himself frustrated by the sense of a hidden lining to her every word. "Ben…"

"I love you Claire." It was if the cork popped.

"I know."

It wasn't the response he'd hoped for. Now she seemed to be lying. She was being slippery; a fish in the shallows that he couldn't spear. He had blurted out his feelings hoping it would force her to drop the facade. Surely, she, who had guessed at his compulsions, would have known that his need for her might have taken many forms, but whether she knew anything about love…oh, the two of them were more alike than she knew!

She continued: "Even though I've broken into your flat?"

"I'm drawn to you all the more for your faults." He saw the surprise, the way her head jolted slightly.

"Charming!" Now she tried to sound coquettish. "What do you mean – *faults?*" She smiled; striving too hard. "Aren't I on a pedestal?"

He got up; she did the same, driven by a very apparent survival instinct. This was not going as he had hoped. Time to put his cards on the table.

"Claire, it's okay. I know about the letters."

"What do you mean?" She flushed.

"That you were planting them yourself."

"I don't…"

He held out a hand towards her. "I said it's okay. I understand."

"You keep saying that. Understand what?"

She was starting to irritate him with this insistence on innocence. *Insistence –innocence – insistence- innocence…time to move on.* He reached into his jacket pocket, withdrew an envelope and extended it to her. When she refused to take it, he opened it anyway, unfolded the letter, read: "See you tomorrow." Now he turned the letter for her to see. "I know you recognise the paper and the printed letter."

Logan took pleasure now from knowing she couldn't read him. It made a change!

"Like I said," he continued, "I understand…that it was a cry for help. That you needed the attention; the protection. Needed me." He took a careful step forward, hand reaching for her again. "We're damaged goods, Claire. We belong together."

He could see some weight lifting from her shoulders for a moment, but it seemed to settle again.

"How are you damaged, Ben?" Now she stepped towards him. "What have you done that's worse than sending yourself anonymous, threatening letters and wasting police time?"

He couldn't decide whether or not the question was rhetorical, but it was rendered immaterial as, with a sudden, but gentle movement, she took his hand. He realised she, too, was offering him an opportunity. His heart started to race. Could he trust the woman who had stolen his key and broken into his apartment? Perhaps that was the very reason he could.

He paused just a moment longer, the diver on the high-board, then said: "I planted the evidence that finally got Jack Geddis convicted."

She withdrew her hand – it might as well have held a twisting blade, such was the pain that involuntary movement caused him. "You mean…he wasn't…"

"Guilty? Not of attacking you. But he's a bad man. Society was better off with him behind bars. So, I took some fibres from the matting of his classic car and switched them with the non-incriminating ones we had in the evidence store. You remember the fibres?

She didn't respond; backed away a step or two.

"Don't go cold on me, Claire. I did it for you."

"For me? You locked up an innocent man for me?"

"But hasn't it given you at least some peace of mind?"

Her eyes blazed and the flame singed him. "Peace of mind?" she spat. "Oh sure, there might have been a moment's relief, but I was never so foolish as to think Jack Geddis might be the one-and-only sexual deviant out there. I felt unclean; unsafe. How do you think I feel now – an innocent man…?"

"He's not innocent – he's…"

"He is of *this* crime!" she shouted.

"He's a disgusting worm, Claire, who deserves…well actually, he's getting better than he deserves."

"But did he deserve to die? And God knows what it says about you that you could kill a man you knew?"

He stopped, astonished. "What do you mean?"

She pointed towards the bedroom. "I looked in your book… your journal…whatever it is. You knew him years ago."

He felt himself turn cold. "No, I meant what did you mean about me killing him?"

The thermostat was definitely turned down, because now she seemed to freeze. "What…" she stumbled over her words, "…I thought you said you were going to kill him."

"I never said that." He saw her jaw drop and knew it mirrored his own – and then things clicked into place. "Ah; you mean when I said he would never bother you again – it was ok that I killed him when you thought he was guilty. Boy, was I right, Claire – you are damaged goods."

She turned her back to him and he walked across to her, putting his hands on her shoulders. She tensed and shrugged at his touch, leaving him feeling betrayed; by her and by his need for her.

"Claire, it's still ok. I want you – more than ever. We can get through this together, if we can just be honest with each other… and ourselves."

"What, even though my actual attacker is still out there?"

He turned her to face him. "You've got me to protect you."

His hand lifted her chin. "We're a match made in hell, Claire." There was fear in her eyes. "I mean, look at you, in all your bargain basement clothes; hoping I'd never know you'd been here. You're a quick learner in the ways of deception. I agree with you, when you say you found what you wanted. And I think you didn't even know what it was you were looking for till you found it. It's got a lot of names." She was starting to shake. "Excitement... deceit... power. I think as you broke in and went through my things, the sense of intrusion brought you to within a step of being thrilled. And you were wondering; *is this what my attacker felt; this sense of taking; the power of being where you have no right?*"

The quivering of her body was starting to excite him and his own pulsed with expectation as she looked him deep in the eyes, and said:

"Yes, Ben, I found what I needed."

20

"Mrs Shanklin…is Claire here?"

"Freddy! What a pleasant surprise. No, she hasn't been by yet. Said she had an errand to run first." The middle-aged version of Claire – the hair was shorter and a skilful mix of ash-blonde and grey, but otherwise the genes were unmistakable in the intelligent pretti-ness of the eyes and the flawless complexion – smiled and waved a gesture of welcome. "Won't you come in? I've just put the kettle on."

"No, thank you; I…" Freddy stopped as something occurred to him. "Is Cissie still here?"

"Yes, she is." Mrs Shanklin's smile transmuted into a frown. "Poor mite."

"Another nightmare?"

"I'm afraid so. Claire's very concerned; so much so, she's even left these."

She reached across to a little table by the door and picked up some pills.

Freddy examined the packet. "These are old-style antihis-tamines." He looked at Mrs Shanklin with concern. "In other words, off-label sleeping pills. Wow!"

"Yes, that's the first time I've ever known Claire to consider it." She shook her head. "You remember she wouldn't even take any pills herself during the pregnancy. But she said enough is enough. Of course, there's no way I would even consider giving these to a little child." Mrs Shanklin seemed to stare into nowhere. "She really didn't seem herself – Claire, I mean."

"You know what. I think I'll take you up on that cup of tea after all."

The smile returned. "Delighted. Come in."

Cissie was at the breakfast table, ploughing into her honey-nut cornflakes with a gusto that belied the dark circles under her eyes.

"Hello Uncle Freddy."

"Hi Cissie. Grandma tells me you had another bad dream."

He saw a frisson of annoyance cross Mrs Shanklin's face. At first he wondered whether it was the *grandma* reference, given that Mrs Shanklin's figure and demeanour belied her years; it was evident Claire owed her stunning looks to her mother's DNA. But on second glance, as she shook her head at him, he believed it was the reminder of the nightmares. Still, he didn't have time for such sensitivities now and carried on regardless.

"I think I can help you."

"Good." Cissie turned to her cornflakes again, displaying the misleading resilience of childhood.

"But I'm just going to get a cup of tea first." *And a telling off,* he predicted in silence.

****

"I assure you it will do her no harm – it didn't the last time; in fact, best case scenario, I get to the root of what's frightening her and banish it.

"Best case scenario? You mean there's a worst case?" Mrs Shanklin's look could have – best case scenario – been described as dubious at the prospect of the darkest corners of her grandchild's fledgling mind being probed. "But hypnosis, Freddy – it's out of the question. One hears so many bad things."

He knew he had to stand up to her. "Does one? May I ask when the last time was that you discussed this with friends or met someone who'd experienced anything like this at first hand?" Mrs Shanklin remained silent. "I suspect there are a few too many publicity-hungry mountebanks on the TV, or Hollywood script-writers influencing public opinion on the topic. But the last time, it actually helped us to understand the potential source of the dreams."

"Didn't prevent them though, did it?"

"Actually it did help Claire to find a means. She was making some progress until…" He stopped, not wanting to discuss his concerns and add to the woman's worries. "But look, I won't do it without your permission."

Mrs Shanklin clutched her tea mug in both hands. "Can't we wait till she comes back?"

"I'd rather not."

He saw the questioning look in her eyes and reached a decision. Time was of the essence here; it didn't allow for playing games. Freddy continued:

"Ok, Mrs Shanklin, the fact is I think Claire may be in danger," – he saw her stiffen – "and this might help her."

"But how? I don't understand. What danger?"

Freddy sipped his tea, watched two specks of less-than-fresh milk spinning on the top while he gathered his thoughts and sought to reduce the complexities. "Ok, I'm not sure I fully understand it myself, but I believe, during the traumatic months that followed the attack on Claire – when she refused to take sedatives because she feared they might harm her unborn child – the horrendous nightmares that she herself was experiencing transmitted themselves somehow, at a subliminal level, to Cissie, forming some sort of psychic link with the attack, or at least with the trauma of it. Then, since Richard disappeared – died as it now turns out, which makes more sense in a way – I believe he has been trying to communicate something through Cissie," he shrugged in slight embarrassment, as if he could not quite believe he was propounding this theory, "about the nature of his death perhaps, or some imminent danger resulting from it."

He could see the impact of this on Mrs Shanklin. Her next question suggested a willingness to put cynicism to one side, but not forever. "How do you know it's Richard who's trying to communicate – if I can believe any of this?"

"Because the nightmares started the day he disappeared, which seems likely to be the day he died. It's been assumed it was an accident – the whole scene suggests as much. But who knows? I'm not one hundred percent sure why he was heading off in that direction. Either way, Cissie knew nothing about his disappearance and he had been away from home before for long periods. So; coincidence or not?" He considered. "And I don't know whether Claire told you this, but the expression being used by the advancing shadow in Cissie's nightmares is *nice and easy;* the first words Claire's attacker whispered to her from the back of the car and which she had blocked out subconsciously from that day as a result of the trauma. Clearly our little girl in there has psychic channels open."

Mrs Shanklin put her hand to her chest. "My God!"

"That expression must have been lurking in the shadows of Claire's nightmares. It's a hook in Cissie's mind and her father is grasping at it, perhaps to warn her, or Claire, that *something wicked this way comes.* One of the features of Cissie's nightmares seems to be something getting ever closer. Why don't you let me see if I can find out what it is, and if I can help? My fear is that that wickedness has its claws in Claire even as we speak."

****

"She's under."

"So quickly," whispered Mrs Shanklin.

Like daughter, like mother, thought Freddy as Mrs Shanklin repeated Claire's exact words from the previous hypnosis session.

"Always easier with a young mind. There's no need to whisper, by the way."

As if adding dramatic effect for Mrs Shanklin's benefit, another squall of rain slapped against the window. The weather had comprised interplaying dappled sunlight and shadows all morning.

"Can you hear me Cissie?"

"Yes." A dreamy voice; like something out of a film, thought Freddy, though without warmth.

"Where are you?"

"Nowhere?"

Fantastic; she'd returned straight away; the place seemed to lie waiting on the other side of the subconscious' automatic door and she needed only to wander within range of the sensors. "And is Nowhere as pretty as ever?" Silence. "Cissie?"

"I can't tell."

"Why not, Cissie?"

"Mummy's built a wall."

"Shall we take a look over the wall?"

"No."

"Why not?"

"It's waiting."

Freddy glanced at Mrs Shanklin. "What's waiting, Cissie?"

"The shadow. It's on the other side of the wall. We're safe behind the wall."

Freddy didn't know whether he was doing the right thing, but time was pressing; he could feel it. "Cissie, let's have a look over the wall."

He heard Mrs Shanklin stir, concerned.

"I don't want to."

"We're safe. We don't have to go over the wall."

"I don't want to!"

"Cissie?"

"Yes?"

"If we don't look, then the thing will just wait there, and wait and wait. But if we look, I promise I'll make it go away." Freddy chewed on his bottom lip; he wasn't sure that promise had been a wise move, but he had to throw the dice; he was sure Claire's life depended on it. He had other concerns too, but didn't fully understand them yet; they remained ghosts on the edge of his vision.

The little girl was deep in thought. Then she said: "I'm scared."

"I'll protect you." Another pause. "Cissie…" Insistent.

"Ok."

Freddy did not dare look at Mrs Shanklin; he knew her eyes would be accusing him. Instead, he concentrated on the girl. "Right; I'm lifting you up now. Steady as it goes. Are you ok?"

Cissie swayed in her seat. "I'm ok."

"Can you see anything?"

"Not yet."

Suddenly the girl stiffened. She gasped.

And the strangest thing happened; a smile broke out on her face. "Hello." Now she blinked and tears rolled down her cheeks – refugees from the world that lay on the other side of her hypnotism – and she gave a little wave, as children do from boats and train windows to strangers.

Now Freddy did look around at Mrs Shanklin, needing a partner in his lonely confusion. She was biting her bottom lip. "Who did she see?" she asked.

He turned back to Cissie. "Who was it, sweetheart?"

21

"Damn! Damn and fuck!" He hammered the heel of his palm against the steering wheel again. "You should have seen it Freddy, you should have seen it. Call yourself a psychologist? Ghost-buster would be a better description – you've been chasing phantoms."

He threw the car round the next corner, the shrill squealing of the tyres somehow in keeping with the cacophony in his head, and then just as swiftly screeched to a halt. Was this the place? Forest Avenue, Heath had said on the phone – sounded appropriate too, given the place where Claire had been subjected to her terrible ordeal. Remembering the flat number was no problem; 17 – a prime number, it had stuck in his head. He'd not had to call in any favours to get the details from Heath on the phone a few minutes before, but he'd picked the officer for a reason, knowing there was no love lost between him and Logan.

As he rushed up the stairs he wasn't sure quite what he was going to do, but as long as he was in time to prevent something bad, it didn't matter.

He hammered on the door; no reply – on reflection not such a surprise, was it? Under the circumstances he was hardly going to get a response. That was when it occurred to him that he hadn't seen Claire's vehicle outside. That could mean one of two things. Either way, it also meant he might be too late.

"Maybe she's gone back home," he muttered to himself, only really voicing the thought so he could reject it – one less unwanted guest in his overcrowded brain. Under other circumstances, he might have tried calling her mobile, but he didn't want to risk spooking either of them, which might have had consequences he refused to entertain. Of course there was always the chance that Claire and Logan were in the flat now consummating whatever their disturbed minds mistook for love, but somehow he doubted that, or at least didn't want to dwell on the idea. How soon after Claire had Logan left this morning? What had Heath said – half an hour…ish? Given that, in all probability, they had spent the night together it was unlikely Logan had driven here so they could start all over again. Maybe he had just headed straight to work at the police station. That made most sense. After all, the plain-clothes officers had said Claire allowed him to use the shower; why would he head home?

None of this reasoning made a damn difference. He needed facts, not conjecture.

Which was when it struck him that the proof he needed might be waiting just around the corner – literally.

Freddy took the stairs down to the foyer three at a time and crashed back out onto the road. He leapt into the car, drove around the block and saw his worst fears encapsulated in the hard, sleek shape of Claire's Volvo S60.

"They've gone in *his* car," he hissed. "A nice twist." Freddy pressed his lips together in anger and spat his next words: "What the fuck are you talking about, *a nice twist?* This isn't some Agatha Christie plot. Get moving!"

He floored the accelerator and roared away, hoping that his gut instinct was correct, while praying that it wasn't; unsure who was in the greater danger of damnation – Claire or Logan.

****

For the entire time they had been talking in the aseptic prison-cell that was Logan's apartment, Claire had had to fight the urge to bolt for the door, but she knew he was coiled tight, ready to spring out and bar her way. Anyway, it was doubtful her shaking legs would have been up to it. She knew she would have to garner her reserves of strength for the only option left to her.

That it should come to this. Could she go through with it?

She forced herself to remember.

A stormy night; her naked, shivering body, bound at wrists and ankles; the smell of the sack over her head, and of her own urine; not knowing whether she will live or die, but believing the latter; the approaching footfall; the bestial groan in her ear; the knife, so sharp that its touch on her shoulder is almost imperceptible; the disgusting warmth and stench as the contents of her bowels run down her legs.

And he had the nerve to call her damaged goods.

Yes, she could go through with it. Living with it might be another matter, but when the doubts and tormenting thoughts came, she would try to remember that everything passes; that even the threatening howl of the wind in the trees on that horrible night six years ago had become the locomotive breath of freedom and release.

Her eyes were closed and, once again, she heard the sound of approaching feet. She felt his hands on her shoulders and she tensed at the touch, but why should she care now whether she hurt his feelings? For all she knew, he was, after all, the very author of her despair. As he spoke, she listened hard for any clue in his voice, but guessed that if it *had* been him in the car that night, she would have picked it up by now; in some nuance or inflexion; in an unguarded syllable at an intimate moment – or during their sexual frenzy, as she had offered her wrists to be tied. She had seen excitement and darkness in his eyes – seen that they were too alike ever to have survived each other – but not guilt. Not that any of that – *any* of it – mattered any more. The disgusting images on the memory stick were reason enough to take action. She shuddered as she thought of his stained hands on her flesh; his defiling cock entering her body, which was no temple, but had so recently played host to an act of desecration. Oh, the thoughts that must have rampaged through his head as he…

She stopped herself. Keeping control was all.

Now it was his lips pressing hard on hers, and then his arousal stiffened against her stomach. And she looked into his eyes, wanting to see the surprise register as she replaced his hard length with one of her own.

"Like I said, Ben, I found what I needed. Now back away or, believe me, I will use it."

He retreated, and she kept the gun – his gun – levelled on him.

"Claire." He held his hands, palms outwards, but said nothing more.

She looked down at the silencer, surprised how steady the weapon was in her hand. "One of a number of things I found in your drawer." She gave an arch smile, which felt forced and must have looked cruel. "Is it the extra length, or the silence that turns you on? Bet you think it's both for me."

"Claire…". His vocabulary seemed to have condensed to one word for the moment.

"Why did you frame Jack Geddis?"

"Like I said, I wanted to give you peace of mind."

"And like I said, you've failed, because I know my attacker is still out there." She looked hard at him. "You call Geddis filth; I looked at that little home entertainment memory stick of yours. You disgust me."

Logan looked puzzled, then aghast. "What? No…no Claire… that was *his,* Claire – I swear it."

"I've taken you at your word before and look where it's brought us – me pointing a gun at someone for the first time in my life. As you said, I'm damaged goods."

"I didn't mean…"

She ignored him. "Why did you keep it…the memory stick… that filth?"

"An insurance policy."

"An insurance policy?" She frowned, but then her eyes widened and she tapped the gun backwards and forwards in the air in mock-enlightenment. "Oh I see; in case he ever came back. And why would he do that?"

"Claire…"

He took a step forward and she raised the gun again. "Back off!"

"I love you."

"You *want* me – that's all."

"I want to protect you; save you. All I've ever done has been to that end."

Claire said nothing for a moment; fought to keep her lips from trembling. It was tough trying to pretend you were hard. But there was no preventing the scalding tears that matted in her eyelashes as she blinked.

"The words are very similar," she said.

"What?" He looked blank.

"Protect and possess."

"I loved you…wanted you, yes…but loved you from the moment I saw you."

"Where was that exactly? In the car park of the ante-natal clinic?"

"No!" His irritation seemed genuine enough. "And you know that's not true, so stop trying to trick me. When I was assigned to your case." Now his eyes were starting to fill up, maybe through frustration as much as fear, but she couldn't tell. "You looked so vulnerable, yet somehow it made you so much more beautiful. I couldn't begin to imagine what you'd just gone through."

"Well, let's put that right, shall we?"

"What do you mean?"

It was time to act. The more she let him talk, the weaker her resolve would be. She gestured towards the door with the gun; the movement so alien to her that she felt she had wandered into someone else's movie.

"Let's go for a ride."

****

The enforced change of plan meant they had to drive round the block to her car, where she collected one essential item from the boot. He didn't attempt to drive off; she guessed the look in her eyes told him she meant business. Perhaps even more persuasive was the memory stick in her pocket. There would be nowhere to go – nowhere to hide – if he pissed her off enough to make her use it against him.

They drove out of town, riding in silence at first; each with their own reason for not wanting to speak, but both fearing the misplaced word which might break the tenuous link of humanity that still held them.

"Left here," she said at last, "though maybe I don't need to tell you that."

"Jesus, Claire!" There was a catch in his voice; he seemed on the verge of despair.

She, on the other hand, felt calm – surprisingly so – and didn't have to fight any debilitating she-demons threatening her strength; all she needed was to remind herself of the smell of fear and help-lessness, a fusty odour of panting breath on woven sacking, and any weakening of her resolve fled.

Logan lifted his hands from the steering-wheel as he protested and Claire emphasised the fact that she was pointing the gun at his genitals. "Keep your hands on the wheel."

The day was wearing its storm-cloak again, pulled tight around it now, so that the track looked much as it had on that terrible evening of her ordeal, as they at last neared the destination.

"I see you remember the way to the quarry," she said.

"Of course I do; I was handling the case, Claire. I've visited this site more than once."

They took the turning and as they headed deeper into the darkness of the woods, it seemed Ben Logan was ever closer to breaking.

"Why, Claire; why have we come here?"

"For Auld Lang Syne?"

"For fuck's sake, Claire, I didn't do it! I wasn't around when it happened."

They had reached the yard in front of the Portakabin. Claire reflected: "You know what; I know – and it actually doesn't matter. And you can stop repeating my name. They might train you in the police to build a bond that way, but – remember – familiarity breeds contempt. Now please, get out of the car."

As they walked through the trees – bare branches mimicking the wooden clatter of lances at a jousting tournament – Claire's unexpected calmness held; a defence mechanism keeping the demons at bay, enabling her to deal both with the memories and with the sight of Logan – head bowed, breathing ragged – either of which might have broken her before. She couldn't afford to break. Someone had to pay for driving her this close to madness.

"Perfect weather for it, Ben."

He said nothing, ignoring her mocking use of his name.

At length they reached the spot where it had all happened, as far as she could remember.

"Strip off."

"Claire, please…"

"Strip!"

As he turned his back – an almost comical instinct of modesty given their recent enjoyment of each other's' bodies – she shut her eyes for a moment. It was enough; too much. In the drowning wind it seemed her brain would always hold a memory of this place, where one act of cruelty flayed her of the life she had known and scarred the days she had left.

She opened her eyes in time to see Logan removing the last of his clothes. As he turned, she noticed the chill air had transformed the mighty weapon he'd been pressing against her less than an hour before; it wasn't so fearsome any more.

"Put this over your head." She threw him the orange linen supermarket bag, which she had collected from the boot of her car, and pointed to the tie he'd discarded. "Fasten it around your neck."

"Claire, please. Why are you doing this? I thought we had something…"

"Do it."

The fixity of purpose was really something she had never known before. She seemed to have stepped outside herself and allowed a vengeful goddess to take her place while she floated above the scene, calm and detached, watching this ridiculous dumb-show of a woman with a gun and a naked man with an orange bag over his head. She wanted to laugh; had to stifle it for her own sake – it might have sounded too much like insanity. Below her…

…*the woman forces the man to kneel, and Claire listens in – except no words are spoken for some time; minutes pass in silence, or rather a period devoid of human interaction; just the wind and the trees argue.*

It seems the man starts to wonder whether he is now alone, because he lifts his hands to remove the bag.

"Leave it!" *barks the woman and he obeys. Now she speaks.*

"You thought, with Richard out of the way, you could just step in and play happy families."

"I swear to you I had nothing to do with his death."

She considers. "No, I know that, although you might have done, if I hadn't beaten you to it." *The man's shoulders stiffen.* "I saw how you looked at him; knew the contempt you felt for him; and how slighted you felt when he refused to accept your invitation to dinner after the case closed. But revenge was only part of your motivation. You were probably gathering evidence to present to me when the time was right. You wanted me and he was in your way. And if he'd treated me right maybe that's where he'd have stayed." She puts the heel of one hand to her eye for a moment. "He should have just loved me."

The woman's gun hand has lowered; the weapon hangs pendulous in her fingers and though her eyes stare ahead, the intense focus is into the past as she continues:

"Things weren't perfect, but they might have mended. What you can't know − what no man can ever know − is how it feels to carry a child; to surrender your body to a man; to invite him in; to feel part of him growing inside you, despite your doubts about your relationship and your ability to be a good mother. Then someone comes along and simply strips you naked − tortures you; defiles you as if you're there for any man who cares to take a piece." Her voice is a paradox, growing strong with anger just as it weakens with other emotion. "And you escape from that horror, only to find yourself questioned; doubted. But still you bear and protect that child; deal with the nightmares…night after night after night…the bad dreams. You cope with it, because you want that child − it is something you have created and it will love you, even though you know the chances of you loving it back as much hang by a slender thread; and still you deal with it. Just as you deal with the eyes of men wandering over your body; their minds gloating over the mental images of your enslavement; knowing some wish they could re-enact it.

"Then there's the pain of child-birth." She frowns. "Just a memory now, but as hard a test as your body will meet in this life − or so I had hoped.

"And through all of this your husband's love should be a beacon of light, guiding you through the shadows. You accept your unexciting marriage because you believe the love and comfort it might now bring will protect you from the images of sexual deviancy that have plagued you. You even fight to resist your own desire for a more exciting physical relationship, which you know is potentially on offer from a lonely and besotted police officer, because you think succumbing to that would lower you to the level of your attacker.

"But your trust is shattered as you begin to suspect that your husband is having an affair. After all you've been through; he's…fucking someone else. Can you even conceive how…" after a pause her voice cracks on the first syllable, "… devastating it is to watch them holding hands, bold as brass, in a cafe? To suspect he's creeping around downstairs in the middle of the night; how it feels to stand halfway down those stairs one night listening to his whispered phone conversation; and how that rage builds while you tiptoe towards him? He's sipping flat champagne from a bottle you shared that evening, his back to you while he says softly: "No, she'd never do that...no, head-case though she is! That's your speciality." He laughs softly; wickedly. "Boy is it. No wonder it's called a dangerous liaison. I do love a business trip." You're about to ask who it is, enjoy the look on his face when he finds he's been caught and you order him to get out – but then he says something, laughing as he does so, and seals a much worse fate than divorce. The memory of those fateful words and the next few moments is just a blur – you open your eyes, unaware you had closed them and look down at the blood-smothered champagne bottle in your hand. Beyond it lies his body, skull smashed in. It's clear he's dead. His words, his laugh seem to have given you strength enough – even in the early hours of the morning when you're at your lowest ebb – to take his life.

She stops for a moment, chest rising and falling as if the physical effort of recalling those events has left her exhausted. As for the man; despite the bag tied over his head, he seems to be listening and intent. His body is still; he senses this is a pivotal moment for his future and behaves like all cornered, scared beasts, remaining motionless.

The woman continues: "You wrap him in a bin bag and blanket. Then starts the tough bit, strange though that might sound from someone who has just taken a life with such brutality. Though he had let himself go in recent years, he had been sporty and his body is big and heavy. Somehow, fear and adrenalin help you to find the strength to drag him through the house to the four-wheel drive, always glancing round towards the stairs, fearing to see the accusing, tiny figure of his daughter standing there. The fear of losing her drives you. The sound of his shattered head bumping and dragging on the floor as you do so and the sight of its contents starting to stain the blanket will fill your dreams forever. It's the early hours; your daughter is fast asleep. This has to succeed, if she's not to wake up to a world in which she's in care, while you languish in prison. Creeping past her room, you try not to glance in. It's been tough enough robbing her of her father without looking at her *sleeping in innocence. You pack your dead husband's overnight bag, pick up his briefcase and put them in the car.*

"There's no-one around, so you head out onto the lonely coastal road. Not for the first time, there's an unwanted, terrifying passenger in your car. Then you divert from the road down a smaller track towards a point where you know the towering cliffs drop sheer below the waterline; a spot where signs warn the unwary that the coast has eroded dangerously. It's considered a haunted spot by some, following the disappearance over the edge decades back of a local girl. The B-road has been re-routed since; few head this way except on foot. Leaving the engine running, you start to try to pull the body onto the driver's seat. Never have you understood the word 'deadweight' more, plus the body's stiffening. Time and again you nearly manage it, only to lose your grip and watch it slide out again. All you want to do at times is drop to the floor and weep, but fear and love – the latter for your daughter, whom you suffered for as you carried her, cried out in pain for when you gave birth and bonded with through the shared terrors of your nightmares – they help you to find strength. You manage to get him into place and shut the door. Panting hard, you glance around, grateful for once that you live in a remote spot. The ruins of an old tin mine are silhouetted against the sky and you imagine ghosts watching you from its shadows. The elements, the wind and the waves rage against your crimes and howl your damnation through fissures in the rocks.

"Now clambering in through the other door, you unwrap him and release the handbrake. He will probably be found, eventually, but he's been away before, so you don't have to report him missing yet. Give it forty-eight hours – it would seem odd if you didn't call the police eventually.

"The champagne bottle didn't even break, and while your daughter continues to sleep there's surprisingly little clearing up to do; just one patch of blood and a bin-bag to wash, and a blanket to burn."

The naked man continues to kneel in silence. He knows now that this woman can kill; worse – that she can plan and lie. Again he must feel that the thread by which his life hangs may snap with a word.

"But you realise something is amiss when your daughter starts to have nightmares. And when under hypnosis she mentions a dragging sound and

a phrase no-one could possibly know – since you yourself had forgotten it – though you don't understand why, you fear the worst, and try to help her build a wall in her dreams, so that she won't see what's on the other side."

****

"And when her psychologist friend hypnotises the little girl once again and sees what's beyond the wall – a female shadow dragging something behind her – he puts two and two together, and finally succeeds in making four. The psychic bond is, and always has been between mother and child. The reason her nightmares started the day her father disappeared is because that's the day her mother killed him."

****

A man's voice. She hasn't heard him approaching – who knows how long he's been standing there at the edge of the clearing – and feels herself tumbling back to the ground.

****

As the gun pointed in his direction Freddy raised his hands.

"No need to shoot, Claire." He stepped forward into the clearing.

"Stop there!"

"Ok." *Keep talking*, he said to himself; *engage her*. "You know, Claire, I can't understand why you ever brought the whole business of Cissie's nightmares to my attention. Surely it would have been better – for you – to have let sleeping dogs lie."

Claire gave an empty smile. "Well that's the irony, isn't it? The dogs wouldn't go to sleep. And it wears you down. At the end of the day, she's my daughter, so maybe I hoped you'd help us find a cure. How was I to know it would open a can of worms? I was just…" she rubbed her eyes as if the memory was already too much, "…so tired."

"You have a restless, intelligent mind, Claire. I believe you might just have been a bit curious too."

"Perhaps I needed to talk – like anyone who's ever killed anyone. But I don't need to now." She pointed the gun back towards Logan's head.

Freddy saw that bagged head spin in his direction.

"For God's sake, help me!"

"Be quiet, Ben Logan – or rather Adam Hammett – if you know what's best for you," said Freddy, seeing from the jerking motion of the captive's head the reaction to the sound of his real name. It was confirmation of what he had guessed.

Claire's gun-arm swivelled back towards Freddy, then to her captive again.

"Adam?…Hammett?"

"It's a long story, Claire."

"So you did know him before. I wondered why you were in his book."

"His book?"

"Oh, your name's not in there, but I recognised the description, the floppy dark hair, the blue eyes, the tweed jacket and brogues, the postures when you listen. Did you know all along Ben Logan, or Adam…whoever was trouble? Why didn't you tell me?"

"I didn't know, I swear. I hadn't yet joined the dots. Like I said, Claire, it's a long story. Let us all live long enough to tell it."

The extended, gun-toting arm continued to swivel; a weather-vane in a mad storm.

Freddie pushed on. The silences were the worst. "It's ok, Claire, no-one's going to try anything. But let him go. His biggest crime has been believing he's in love with, rather than obsessed by you. Not his only one, of course, but the one that almost cost him his life. It was unprofessional, but not worthy of execution."

"You're almost right, Freddy; but I have another use for him."

"I know that now," Freddy shook his head. "Though it took me long enough to work things out. I think my residual feelings for you blinded me for a while." He paused. "As soon as I mentioned to you at the clinic that Jack Geddis was due for release, you changed. You became...remote. And that's when you reached for Logan, wasn't it, through the letters; the threatening letters you sent yourself. You reeled him in."

"Partly; I thought he could protect me; from an innocent man, as it turns out – well, innocent of this crime."

"He's not innocent!" Logan's disembodied voice shook. The irony did not escape Freddy; words and physical movement were things on which Logan, as he chose to think of him despite everything, relied. Now, his face hidden, they were all he had.

"Be quiet." Freddy hated being so harsh to a terrified man but felt any interjection from Logan would simply make things worse.

Claire continued: "The choice of bait was easy; is there any man who can't be won with a fuck?" She nodded – like so many of her actions now the gesture seemed imbued in distraction. "But I'd made a mistake; heard what I wanted to hear. I thought he'd arranged for Geddis to be killed." Freddy fought hard to suppress the shudder that passed through him at the callousness – the iciness – of that statement. Where was the Claire Treloggan he knew? She seemed buried deep. "I thought that was the message he was giving me."

"So, with Geddis out of the way, you no longer needed protection. But long before that you'd also started to panic; that life would still trip you up; that when Richard was found it would all unravel. The body almost always turns up eventually and I can tell by how you're dressed today that Ben would have told you there's usually some forensic evidence to be had. You've probably seen documentaries or dramas about the truth of long-dead cases coming to light through advances in science. You thought you might still be uncovered as Richard's murderer." He saw Claire nod, reliving the thoughts and fears. "And so that second role had emerged, for which Ben seemed perfectly suited; the role of..."

"…scapegoat. Exactly — for that very murder. And no-one would be able to prove I slept with him subsequently. All they would see was a cold plan worthy of a cold fish — remove the rival and win the woman with whom he had become obsessed. The letters too — planted by him, as the only person with access to the house. The officers on watch would be able to verify that no-one else came near. I would be free from suspicion of any ulterior motive." She was smiling now at her own cunning. The sight chilled Freddy, but he forced himself to press on.

"And as a murderer needs a victim, it was you who tipped off the police about where the car might have gone over the cliff." Now Freddy nodded too, as if in appreciation, perhaps awe, of Claire's mendacity.

"There's an interesting photograph under his mattress…" she pointed at Logan with the gun, "…of my deceased husband and his bit on the side holding hands in a café." She gestured towards Logan. "It's proof that he was following them; that he was jealous enough to consider killing Richard."

"I never took a photograph," said Logan, fear and injustice helping him find his voice again, even though it sounded alien and disembodied from inside the bag. "Yes, I was watching what he was doing, and yes, I wanted to warn you. I admit I wanted you, but I took no picture."

"But I did."

Freddy heard a muffled echo of his own gasp come from Logan at this revelation.

Claire continued:

"Originally, I took it just for proof of his unfaithfulness — you know, for when it came to a divorce — but then I guess circumstances and anger overtook me when I…" she paused, pressing again the heel of her palm to her eyes, fighting the softer person betraying her resolve, "…when I heard him tell her he loved her." She regathered herself. "That's one of the reasons I was in your flat today in the first place; to plant it. I'd have found a way to convince the police that your home might be worth checking, perhaps tell them that your attention was getting a bit creepy; that you had made inappropriate comments about Richard, suggesting you'd taken care of a problem for me. And once I was there, the things I discovered presented me with even more ammunition. Your OCD; perfect – a man capable of obsession. The little bag of fibres. They didn't register at first, but when you mentioned about planting evidence I clicked. They'll be quite compelling when the police go through your things, particularly when I tell them you wanted to bring me peace of mind. And talking of the mind, that memory stick will show that yours wasn't too stable. Once I saw the contents of that, your fate was sealed. I realised jail is too good for you. There needed to be justice. So, Plan C came about. Add all those things together, plus your insistence on guarding me in person and the letters you planted while you were on duty…"

"Stop it!" shouted Logan, "stop it! This is insane!"

"Exactly. And I'm sure that's what the investigation will conclude about you after your suicide."

"My what?" There was horror in Logan's voice. He was broken.

"Your body and your deeds will be the silent witnesses to your own madness. Considering how some of you doubted my story…" she looked hard at Freddy, who wanted to protest till he saw the absence of a soul in her eyes, "…how, despite the ligature marks on my wrists and ankles, which the defence lawyer charmingly suggested could have come from some bondage rituals in my private life, there were those who thought I'd invented it all, and was making some grotesque cry for help; all in all they're bound to think that you were here alone with just your insanity for company. Why do you think I didn't ask you to cuff yourself?"

She stepped forward suddenly and the kneeling figure cringed at the sound of her footfall. She continued; her voice still strong. "Yes, they'll think that, having finally claimed your prize, you couldn't live with how you won it; what you'd done to the woman who'd been through hell; someone with whom you'd become obsessed as some sort of trophy, despite the trauma of her recent history. Your mind went and the rest of you followed. You came here, full of guilt and remorse, to re-enact the scene, except this time with yourself as the victim." She came forward again, raised the gun and put it to Logan's head. He shrank at the touch of it; cringed.

Freddy had felt powerless to intervene till now. Something told him this scene had to play itself out; he could make no move towards the firework with the touch-paper lit. But now he needed to act. "Claire!" he shouted. "Don't!"

For the moment she stopped, though she didn't look at him. That was a sign he could not interpret without knowing whether his friend was still in there somewhere.

Freddy played his final card: "He's a victim too. His sister died as a result of Geddis' actions. He told me all about it years ago, but I hadn't made the connection, joined all the dots, until the early hours of this morning. Don't you see, he would never harm you? It was his sister you referenced earlier, who disappeared over the edge of the cliff where you disposed of Richard."

Around them, a silent audience of thousands seemed to be approaching in the sudden patter of rain. Very quickly it grew in intensity, soaking the three of them. Apart from the shaking of Logan's naked, terrified body, they did not move for the duration of the squall which may have lasted a matter of seconds, or minutes. It was a moment of melodramatic absurdity, as if the three of them had reached an unspoken understanding that the whole episode would have to wait for the rain to pass. Freddy felt he might shut his eyes and open them to find none of it had happened. In fact he did close them, but when he looked again, the gun was still pointing at Logan's head.

"Well, I can't now anyway."

It was Claire's voice and the sound of it, deadened and heavy from damp air and an aching heart, broke the spell. Freddy realised that he had been the last one to speak and this was her response; under the circumstances the words sounded almost lame and anti-climactic. He was beginning to wonder whether he had indeed dreamt the rain, when she continued. "That *was* the plan, until another witness showed up." She lowered the gun, turned and looked at Freddy, and the pleading – the return of humanity – in her eyes was almost too much to bear. "And you probably saved me, because you know too much. You understand."

With that she lifted the gun again; this time placing the muzzle under her chin.

"No!!" screamed Freddy, springing forward. Too late; she had pulled the trigger.

There was nothing. Silence. A second or two passed before it registered; before Claire opened her screwed-up eyes, seemingly becoming slowly aware that she had not blown away the top of her head. She looked at the gun as if it had betrayed her, clearly not comprehending what had happened. He saw her register that the safety was still on, but by then Freddy was on her, though the ease with which he wrestled the gun from her hand suggested she had lost the will to live or die.

"I guess I'm not so streetwise after all," she said.

That was when the cork came out and years of fermenting hurt and rage and misery and despair and – perhaps above all – need escaped in a torrent of sobs; djinnis released from the cursed bottle as she buried her head against his chest.

Freddy held her; supporting someone whose very being, whose *need* for being, was dissolving. She wept for all mankind it seemed and occasional syllables – not even fully-formed words – spilled from her lips, washing away in the tears before they could be understood.

"Sshhh." Freddy stroked her hair. He looked over the top of her towards Ben Logan, now standing naked and absurd, clutching a shopping bag and a tie, and felt his own hysteria rise to confront a situation too surreal for any words except perhaps for the guttural utterances coming from the frightened woman in his arms. He signalled with a slight movement of the head that Logan should just pull on his soaked clothes and say nothing.

At last Claire started to make sense. "What have I become? I nearly…" The sobs struck again. "I did…Richard…"

Freddy held her closer still. She was almost insubstantial; made of grief and tears – her body had nothing left.

Logan was dressed now and stood, awkward, in his clinging, wet clothes a few feet from them. Freddy could see he was shaking with shock and the cold.

At some point the sobbing stopped. The storm had passed, but now, as always, began the task of assessing the damage. A muffled voice spoke into Freddy's chest.

"What will become of me?"

He held her close. "I'll take care of you."

"I don't want to be analysed."

"I'll take care of you as a friend."

"They'll lock me up – if not in a prison, then in a hospital." She looked up at him. Her eyes seemed so washed out, it was hard to imagine they had ever been blue? "And Cissie!" She made as if to run. "I have to protect her." Freddy held her tight.

Freddy looked at Logan again as he spoke to her. "That's not going to happen, Claire. Too much water's passed under the bridge; we all know too much. I think this one's going to be laid to rest right here in the forest. Only the three of us will know."

Logan gave a short nod. "I'm good at that." The tone was self-deprecatory in the extreme. It was a comment Freddy was not even going to try to interpret and Logan seemed in no hurry to volunteer an explanation. The two men stared at each other. In a moment of distraction, possibly his mind's attempt to back away from the horrors for a few seconds, he wondered – if he had passed the DCI in the street all these years later, would he have recognised Adam Hammett? It was disconcerting to think that, ever the slave to the coping mechanisms for his prosopagnosia, Logan was probably subconsciously dismantling and filing away the up-to-date appearance of his now partner-in-silence. Breaking the link, Logan turned to Claire. "All I ever wanted to do was to protect you, but I know my physical need for you got in the way. I'll still make sure you're looked after. I admit as well, I got distracted by that filth on Geddis' computer."

"Is that why you didn't bother submitting my psychological profile to the investigation team?" asked Freddy, but not without sympathy. "You knew certain things in there might draw the investigation's fire away from Geddis?"

"As things stood, we didn't have anything that would nail the perpetrator. The blaze in the car destroyed every shred of evidence and Claire had no recall. I thought we could at least nail someone who deserved to do time. Everyone wanted a conviction. I wanted Claire to find some peace."

"So you came up with the fibres."

"Forensically, it was strong. Luckily, so was the desire to catch a bad guy."

Logan went silent and Freddy saw, all of a sudden, both the young DCI's shame and how much the ordeal had taken out of him. "That was misguided of you, Ben. I know you thought you could protect Claire, but the attacker is still out there somewhere. Maybe we'll never know who it is, but you and I owe it to Claire to make sure his shadow never falls across her again."

As Freddy looked down at her, he spotted a wavering image below the surface of the disturbed waters that were Claire's eyes; it might have been gratitude. He continued:

"There's been crime and there's been punishment." He paused. Those words had caused a deep frown from Logan. "What?"

The DCI looked up again, as if returning from a far-off place. "Nothing. The words just brought back a memory."

To an extent, in Logan's troubled features, Freddy had seen a pale reflection of his own guilty mind. A man had died; a man he had never warmed to, but who had had his life taken nonetheless.

Perhaps there had been an element of justice; that man had been unfaithful to his wife after she had been sexually assaulted and was both fragile and disturbed. Who knew how long that affair had lasted – perhaps since before the attack? There was no way she deserved to be jailed. She was already broken. Maybe the French had it right; they believed in the *crime passionnel;* ironically, a term once referenced by a young Adam Hammett in the aftermath of someone else falling from the edge of a cliff into the sea. Nor did Logan truly deserve to have his life ruined by his misguided attempts to help her. He decided to rephrase his comment.

"Okay, then there's been sin and I'm sure there'll be redemption." He meant it for all present. "An end. And then there's Cissie. She needs her mother. C'mon; let's go get her."

Claire turned her wet, pale face towards Freddy and nodded. With that, they started to move away. Then Freddy felt her resist and stop. She was looking at Logan.

"The sign…on the mantelpiece in your flat…it's a misquote, you know."

The Detective Chief Inspector gave a strange smile; almost ironic, as was his rhetorical response.

"You think I don't know? Why do you think it's there? I can't help how I am, but I can make a stand against the order of things; try to impose a little disorder on my world." He gave her a look, both questioning and knowing. "Strange you should think of that now – and that you should notice."

Claire made to move off, and stopped again, before reaching into her coat pocket and removing the memory stick. She handed it to Logan. "Here; maybe you can still impose a little bit of healthy order on the world. I'll leave you to decide how."

Logan held the stick in shaking fingers, then tapped it thoughtfully on his other palm. "I'll take some time over that. I believe my sister is on here too. I wasn't able to recognise her and wasn't sure I wanted to. Somehow I don't believe the world should see that shame."

Claire gave a nod of understanding, then turned and allowed Freddy's consoling arm to guide her away.

****

She had needed to think fast when Freddy arrived, but in the end the solution had been simple. Walking from the quarry with Freddy's support and Logan, chastened but already eager marching behind, she allowed herself a secret smile of triumph for the performance. Their assumption that she was no munitions expert had worked in her favour; all they had seen was her intent to kill herself. She had known well enough that the safety was on; it was a switch pointing at the word "safe", for heaven's sake. Now, the only two men close enough to have ever worked out that she had killed Richard with ice in her veins and crystal clarity in her mind were wound tightly into her web of deceit.

Being men, they might never learn that the price of their obsession with her was that they became so easy to manipulate. If they ever did, it would not be today.

Freddy had leaned into her and, unable to suppress his professional curiosity even in this extreme circumstance, needed to ask: "Forgive me for wondering this, but has the memory of what Richard said to you, the trigger, come back to you at all, er, since…?"

Given how well she knew Freddy, she'd known this question might come, just not so soon. She had been planning to save this for a time their resolve might need strengthening, perhaps even fake her way through Freddy's whole hypnosis rigmarole to let it out. But, under the circumstances, why not now? Yet even with everything that had passed, she found it hard to crane her neck towards Freddy's ear and whisper…then watch as he went pale.

****

On a night bearing a spooky similarity to the one on which it had all started, as high winds battered the Cornish coast and lost souls wailed in frustration through stone relics of abandoned tin mines, the last chance of discovering the identity of Claire's attacker – the hard evidence – disappeared; though no-one sought it any more.

First it had floated through the window of its owner's sinking 4x4 as the vehicle had plunged beneath the waves; a soaking leather briefcase that spiralled several metres downwards before wedging in a rocky crevice. The locked case contained some token balance sheets and a much greater quantity of pornographic magazines, along with a gruesome little disk. Not a piece of cinema to be left lying around at home when you're planning to be away on a supposed business trip; if the woman who was the subject of the recording had known it existed and that images of it in her husband's mind had, for a while, reignited the physical side of their marriage, she might never have recovered. It's also unlikely that Lucy Rankin's partners in the accountancy firm of Lawless, Rankin and Lunn in Liverpool would have been so keen to lunch with her had they known that the perverted blood pulsing beneath her sharp pinstripe suits had been whipped on a regular basis into a sexual fever by watching that little film in the company of its director, her lover.

Then again, they were accountants. Who knew what turned them on?

Lucy Rankin had moved on. It had taken her a little time to deal with the news that her lover had died. Those last words, *"Nice 'n' easy"*, Richard's favoured expression whenever they were about to indulge some of their perversions, followed by the line suddenly going dead had haunted her a while. But she had needs and it salved her conscience a little that at least she wasn't two-timing him.

But now, more than six years later, the underwater swell caused by the passing storm pulled the briefcase free before sending it over its final edge, and it swirled down, to bump along the murky depths where it belonged. With a touch of irony it came to rest not that far from the remnants of a watch belonging to the man who had served time for the crimes on the disk, a conviction for another man's evil rather than his own; a justice that only the fates and the universe can administer,

THE END